A Tale of Scorpions

Fergus Anstock

Published by Clink Street Publishing 2023

Copyright © 2023

First edition.

ISBN:
978-1-915229-89-2 - paperback
978-1-915229-90-8 - ebook

1972 is remembered for many things. Watergate. A bloody Sunday and a bloodier Friday. The atrocity at the Munich Olympics forever overshadowing the mountainous achievements of Mark Spitz. Multiple earthquakes. The shooting of George Wallace.

For some of the residents of Stetchworth, a buzzy London overspill New Town that had developed cuckoo-like from within the nest of the sleepy Hertfordshire countryside that surrounded it, the year became indelibly tattooed on their memories because of another equally disturbing event.

Stetchworth had begun to be built in the early 1950s. A post-war experiment in the creation of new societies forged in the want of a brave new life away from the war damaged cities. In the case of Stetchworth it was populated largely by Londoners eager for a new challenge in the countryside where equal opportunity was sought after and where old class barriers could no longer pertain.

The accommodation offered by the bold Stetchworth Development Corporation was basic but new. There were no private homes at first although eventually the private developers arrived at the invite of the town planners. After all, every New Town and society demanded private housing to satisfy the needs of a burgeoning property-owning class and it was starting to come. Eventually Mrs Thatcher would offer all Stetchworth residents the wonderful life-enhancing privilege of purchasing their own council homes and of course they did. But not just now.

The town had been built along lines and well planted too. Each new neighbourhood had its own recreation ground with football pitches and cricket squares, netball courts and play areas with swings and slides and roundabouts. Each had its own basic shopping area and primary and infant schools. Not many nurseries back then and most mothers were homebound until the youngest reached five years old. All neighbourhoods were linked by the kind of road system only possible where architects had worked from a blank canvas and alongside most roads ran wonderfully safe cycletracks. Each area of housing had interconnected access roads to both front and back of each individual house often with an offroad parking area surrounded by garages, each individually rented by the house occupant and through which or by the side of which access was available to the back garden of the house, for every house had its own back garden.

As he swung his Jaguar MK X around the corner of one such of these roads on his way home from a night out with wife Jo and friends, Tony Blake was in fine relaxed mood. Blake was an East End boy who had been an early mover to the New Town. It had served him well. He was a criminal from a criminal family and had used his physicality, he was a bull of a man, and his inherited ability to place people at unease, to build a place in the hierarchy of the criminal underworld of Stetchworth. His painting and decorating business had thrived amongst the welter of new homes being built. He never went unpaid. He was able to employ a small team of similar men, all loyal to him and the future was bright. Tony had progressed through the ranks of crime. A few small burglaries as a teenager had led to remand centre and as his experience and professionalism grew so did his level of criminal undertaking. A couple of armed robberies had gone undetected and a period of custody pending trial for a major burglary of a fur shop had ended at the Crown Court where a mixture of a clever lawyer and police incompetence had allowed him to walk free. After that he had promised Jo that his criminal days were behind him. The business would support him and she would not have to worry about what he was up to during those many evenings when she was left alone any more. Yes there was nothing he could not sort out one way or another. He had two young children who were healthy and he had status in his own community. Indeed, had the two of them not just been to the prestigious Bowie Club outside Hitchin where he had been treated as a celebrity, given the best table for him and his friends and generally been fawned upon? Were not the outdoor fireworks celebrations at the Club Hombre this Guy Fawkes Night partly sponsored by his firm? Yes, life was good and getting better.

He parked the car, the symbol of his recently acquired standing and glanced over at Jo who had just stirred from the doze she had been in, the result of a little too much wine and the pleasant rhythm of the car. She smiled and began to collect her effects together from around her comfortable leather seat and the dash pocket. He turned off the car and opened his door creating the automatic light. It was dark in the drive and the Bonfire Night celebrations had ended around the town.

Blake jumped out first and straightened his frame. The car door clicked to. He was aware of a rustle in the hedgerow that was planted inside the closeboard fencing that enclosed most of the Stetchworth drives in the area and he turned to face the sound suspecting a local cat. It was his last living movement.

The flash of a shotgun discharge disturbed the silence and Blake was peppered by the shot. He was hit by a torrent of pellets which seared through his jumper and shirt and penetrated his torso from the navel to the throat. The force of the blast spun him round, still erect. Instantaneously the blast from the second hit him in the back propelling him over the side of the car bonnet before he slumped, dead, to the road.

Jo, already screaming, got out of the car and ran to the side of the lifeless body. Lights began to come on in the neighbouring houses and eventually Jo's screams brought others to the scene. Nobody noticed, now over a hundred yards away, a man in a balaclava and black Crombie coat walking purposefully away from the noise with a short black pouch just large enough to cover a broken shotgun under his arm.

Ken Oliver was now 43 and at the peak of his career. He had risen steadily and inexorably through police ranks and was now Chief Superintendent in the Hertfordshire Police. Any serious crime within the county would inevitably come under his scrutiny. He often mused to himself how he had reached the position. He was intelligent, granted, and he had been in the right place at the right time when other serious crimes had been solved earlier in his career. He had been to university unlike a lot of his colleagues, was reasonably well-read and knowledgeable in world affairs. By the standards of his contemporaries, he was a fairly accomplished package and had applied himself diligently and well. He had also, most importantly steered his ship clear of controversy and had no skeletons in his closet. Until now, that was.

He could not believe he had been so stupid. Six months previously he had placed three of his detectives to carry out surveillance on the National Westminster Bank in Watford. There had been information from a reliable informant that there would be an armed raid on the bank. The exact time and date of the planned robbery had been leaked to the police and the purpose of the surveillance was to establish evidence of the gang involved checking out the premises on a daily basis prior to the raid to ensure that no hidden impediments like roadworks or major staff changes had occurred which might throw the plans of the robbers into disarray. It was a routine surveillance for his team and he had felt no discomfort when they reported in that nothing had been observed on the first two days.

Nor did his antennae flicker too much when he was advised ten days later that Bill Ryan, one of his team at the Watford bank, had been arrested for suspected importuning at a men's urinals in Enfield town centre. The evidence against Bill was some flimsy identification from a member of the public who had said he recognised him as a detective from a road traffic accident some years previous. Bill had never been on road traffic, Oliver had known him for over ten years along with his wife and family and he regarded the incident as totally ludicrous. Moreover his team had confirmed that Bill had been on observation at the very time of the alleged incident. Fortified by this, Oliver had personally intervened with the Enfield investigating officer and in the strongest terms had pulled rank to have the investigation stopped.

"I can assure you from personal knowledge," he recalled himself saying, "that this is a lot of bollocks, if you'll pardon the expression. Bill is the least likely homosexual in the world and moreover I know personally that he was on duty in Watford observing bank robbers for me at the time your witness has him flashing his dick in Enfield. I can personally vouch for his alibi."

How he regretted those words now. The bank robbery had taken place and the robbers nicked at the scene of the crime. It was a coup for the squad involved and the surveillance officers including Ryan had basked in the glow of a job well done even if their real contribution had been minimal. A week later a large brown envelope had fallen through the letterbox at home. Inside were clear large photographs of Bill Ryan entering the men's toilets in Enfield. Other photographs showed a sequence taken from outside which clearly demonstrated a number of men entering after him and exiting before him. He had clearly spent some considerable time inside and the final photos showed him emerging obviously flustered and with the discredited witness immediately behind him.

Oliver tried to rationalize. It was another day perhaps. There was a sensible explanation perhaps but he was too experienced an officer for that. The ramifications were obvious. He had been lied to by his own men and worse he had compromised his own reputation on their say so. He sank to his chair and pondered on what to do next but he had little time to think as, almost immediately, his phone rang just by him.

"Detective Chief Superintendent Oliver?" an Irish accent enquired.

"Who's speaking?" asked Oliver, already aware that this was no ordinary call. He was ex-directory and only his office had the number. Home was sanctuary for all senior police officers and access to telephone numbers and addresses was fiercely guarded.

"You'll have seen the photographs by now," said the voice and continued "and you'll probably already be wondering where your officers really were that afternoon. Now listen to me." He paused

"I'm listening," snapped Oliver, "and I want to know how you got this number."

"Don't let that be your concern, Mister Oliver. Listen to me quite carefully and without interrupting. This will all go away quietly if you do what I tell you."

The Irishman paused again before continuing, sure he had Oliver's attention.

"There will be a disposal on November 5th in Stetchworth. Shortly afterwards you will be told who made the disposal and who you will prosecute. Do you understand?"

"Of course I don't bloody understand," blurted Oliver, immediately regretting the loss of sangfroid. "Who are you and what are you talking about?"

The Irish voice was unruffled and began again.

"You're an intelligent man. You know what those photographs mean for your future and you surely already know that we have a lot more information about you and your force. But we're not interested in hurting you. We simply want you to ensure the disposal is properly disposed of, if you get my drift. Just do as you are told and you will never hear from me again."

The line went dead.

Oliver slumped back into his chair and tried to piece things together. Something bad was about to happen. He had no idea what. Who used the term disposal? What did it mean? Who was this person that seemed to be telling him how to do his job? It could only be serious crime or the IRA. But why would the IRA be in Stetchworth? Surely not a bomb on Guy Fawkes Night. But maybe. 'Disposal' was a word associated with 'bomb' but he could not see the logic and all his knowledge of the IRA told him that there would be no advance warning until an hour before the planned explosion, and that after any atrocity the Republicans would issue a notice claiming responsibility. They never offered up a victim to be prosecuted.

By the end of the night on November 5th the phone call had cost the Hertfordshire Police Force more than £100,000 in manpower deployment costs to provide extra if discreet security at the various firework displays around the Stetchworth area. However there had been little to report by way of incident beyond the usual few fire and firework casualties that were expected at the local hospital on this night every year, a few brawls, customary for Stetchworth gatherings and one or two isolated pickpockettings.

Oliver put his phone down and poured himself a glass of his favourite scotch. He was relieved. His greatest fear had not been realized and the call he had just taken from the station sergeant at the main station in Stetchworth who had been coordinating all security had reassured him that the threatened event had not taken place. Strange things happen in the world of policing and criminals were never reliable advisers of what would happen in the future. He relaxed, read over his agenda for the following day and eventually made his way upstairs where Pam, his wife of 15 years, and two children were already asleep. He crept between the sheets and took a moment to ponder. Perhaps his renowned luck was going to hold and the threatened embarrassment to his life was not going to occur after all.

He heard the phone downstairs at about 3 am. Slowly he regained wakefulness and by the time he had taken his second step out of the bedroom the sickening pangs of anxiety were pulling at him. The voice at the other end of the line was the same one that had allowed him a few hours of restful sleep.

"Hello, boss. I'm afraid we've had a killing in Stetchworth."

"Do we know the victim?" Police routine took over.

"Yes, an old friend of yours, boss, Tony Blake."

"Fucking hell, how?" asked Oliver. He'd crossed swords with Blake on a number of occasions and had him down for the Cortina fur shop robbery but had not been able to do him for it, courtesy of some dreadful work by his men. He was a gangster. Oliver did not know to what extent his level of crime extended but knew Blake had a fearful hold over many of the worst criminals in and around Stetchworth.

"The officers at scene of crime say it looks like two 12-bore blasts as he got out of his car. Messy but professional. He was with his wife Jo but nobody else hurt, boss. No witnesses. Very dead."

"Ok, I'll come straight in. See you in 40 minutes." He placed the phone back and looked up to see Pam in her dressing gown.

"Killing in Stetchworth, I'll have to go in. Go on back to bed."

She smiled. He knew that she couldn't do that. That years of living with him meant that she knew that he would now be a man possessed until the case was more or less solved and that the whole family would be living the drama collectively. He could never switch off.

"Right," she said, "call me mid-morning and let me know what to expect so I can arrange the diary. We've a few things booked this week…"

By 7 am Oliver had a fair idea of what had happened. He had seen the first polaroids from the Scenes of Crime party and had a fair idea in his mind of what had happened. The killer had lain in wait for Blake to return home from the Bowie Club. He had probably had information that Blake was on his way and knew how the car would be parked when Blake drew into the area. Conveniently there was a beech hedge around the fence where the killer could secrete himself. The first blast would have caught him full on from no more than five yards and almost certainly killed him. Blake's strength had kept him upright enough as he spun round to catch the full second blast too. There was no surviving two shotgun blasts like that.

By the time dawn broke that November morning Oliver also knew that the list of men with grievances against Tony Blake was as long as his arm and most of those on the list were capable of severe violence.

He had also learned from his Firearms Officer that it would be almost impossible to identify the weapon that had carried out the assault. Shotgun barrels by their very nature did not leave a fingerprint on the shot they expelled, and whilst under a controlled experiment it might be possible to link a shotgun to shots fired from it by the distribution and pattern of the cartridge wadding expelled from the barrels, it was doubtful at best and Oliver suspected that the activity at the scene would probably have destroyed any worthwhile evidence in that regard.

It had to be a revenge killing of some sort, Oliver reasoned. Blake was a dislikeable man and one of those London criminals who had come up the pecking order by dint of threats and violence. He was a man who demanded his own way in things and had an arrogance about him created by others living in fear of him. He must have pushed one of the local hoods too far and the killing either done by the very man he had frightened or one of his paid cohorts. Word would be out on the street fairly quickly as to who was the likely shooter. This wasn't a hit. Paid hits from London were never carried out by shotgun, always an untraceable revolver which could be disposed of. Shotguns whether sawn-off or not were too bulky and usually carried a history. No, this was local.

At the 8 am briefing he had most of the bleary-eyed officers he wanted on this case in front of him. Whilst it was not a great loss to the community Blake's death nonetheless was an affront to the forces of Law and Order. His team were briefed on Oliver's suspicions, told in no uncertain terms that this was to be investigated as thoroughly as though the victim had been an upstanding member of the Stetchworth community and told to get amongst the local criminal community immediately for any rumours and gossip as to the likely perpetrator.

At 9 am the phone rang on his desk. It was his secretary.

"A man to speak to you, won't give a name, says it's in connection with Tony Blake…"

"Put him through."

He recognized the tone and accent immediately.

"Now, Detective Chief Superintendent Oliver, you know who this is and I warned you that I would be in touch with you again. Listen carefully. The person you will prosecute for the murder of our dear Mr. Blake is one Patrick Crehan. He is known to you. When he is found guilty of this dreadful crime – and DCS Oliver you had better make sure that he is found guilty – then the other matter that we discussed will be completely forgotten about. I don't really need to tell you what will happen if this does not take place, now do I?"

"This is ridiculous," Oliver retorted. "We do not prosecute men on no evidence at the suggestion of an anonymous phone call. We are a police force and investigate matters properly…"

He was cut off in the middle of his sentence by the voice.

"No more, Oliver, you will do as I tell you. You will find the evidence. We are watching you." The phone died.

It was a warm July morning seven months later and Pat Crehan, stylishly dressed in a dark blue suit with a neatly ironed light blue shirt and navy tie appeared calm in the dock at St Albans Crown Court. He had been brought up from Brixton Prison early that morning and been allowed to meet with his wife Bridget who handed him his lovingly pressed clothes to enable him to look at his best during the ordeal of the Crown Court trial that he was about to endure.

Bridget, or 'B' as Crehan and all who knew her called her would follow the same ritual every day throughout the trial. Each day she would attend with a fresh shirt and every third day with a different clean suit. Every evening, before her Pat met with his legal team, he would change in his cell back into his prison clothes, for him as he was on remand, some tracksuit bottoms and a light pullover, and she would take away the daywear for a pressing and a fresh shirt.

B was a teaching assistant at a local Stetchworth primary school. She was an attractive woman of about five feet seven and was one of those people that as soon as you saw them you realized she was of a kindly disposition. She had met and married Pat seven years previously. She had been happy in the marriage although she feared that Pat mixed with the wrong sorts. Nevertheless he had provided for her and the two little girls she had borne him. He was a painter and decorator by trade and seemed to be able to find paying work constantly enough for their needs. They lived in a small three-bedroom council house on the corner of a small square of such houses called Elm Square with a small front garden and a passageway that went around the house to the back door which fronted on a neat back garden and a small garden shed, identical to all of the other corner houses on the square.

A lot had happened to disrupt their lives together in those last seven months.

The pounding on the door at six o'clock in the morning on that fateful day on 9th November had signalled the end of their lives as they knew them. Crehan knew that the noise could only mean one thing and told a drowsy B to tend to the children who must have been terrified. A glimpse through the curtains showed at least three police cars with lights flashing. This was not a polite enquiry.

He shouted that he was on his way to the door. No reason to give them the excuse to batter down the door. Once opened, the door was forced wide open and before any words were spoken three burly detectives were upon Crehan and had him pinned facing the wall.

"What the fuck's this about?" shouted Crehan.

"You know what it's about Crehan, you're fucking nicked. Get him cuffed."

He soon knew. He was bundled into the leading car and within ten minutes was in the entrance foyer of the Stetchworth Police Station where almost the first words he heard were "Patrick James Crehan, you are charged that on or about 2 am on November 6th 1972 you did unlawfully murder Anthony Terrence Blake. Anything you say will be taken down and may be used in evidence against you. Do you understand?"

"You're having a laugh," was all Crehan could hear himself saying. "I was a friend of Tony's. Why would I kill him? Who the fuck says I did?"

He was manhandled through the door which he knew from previous bitter experience led to the line of cells at the station. As he was thrown through the door of the first one, he just had the presence of mind to shout out what he had been thinking throughout the last 20 or so cataclysmic minutes.

"Get me Geoffrey, do you hear, get me Geoffrey."

Although Patrick did not know it, Geoffrey was already on his way to the station. Geoffrey was in fact Geoffrey Chambers , the senior partner of the well-known Hertfordshire solicitors Bletsoe, White and Richards. Chambers had been with the firm all of his professional career and had served his articles under the former senior partner, Maurice Abraham, a towering figure in the local legal fraternity and a criminal lawyer himself. Chambers, now in his mid-thirties had taken on the mantle left by the retirement of his principal and over the last seven or eight years had himself built a reputation as the sharpest criminal solicitor-advocate in the county.

Tall and athletic with an acerbic wit and possessed of huge energy, it came as no surprise to any onlooker that he quickly had a huge following from both his devoted staff and the criminal community who discovered in him a man who could be brutal in his assessment of their chances of avoiding prosecution when guilty but also passionate in his defence of them when he felt they were either innocent or had been badly treated. By the early 70s it was nothing for Chambers to be appearing in several different courts on multiple cases most days of the week. He travelled between appointments in a brown Triumph Vitesse. He was a fast driver too with advanced test skills and the Vitesse, effectively a Herald with chrome bumpers and a two-litre engine, was known around the courts and to many of the county's traffic police.

The gateway to Chambers was his highly accomplished secretary, Nora Peach. Nora was a forbidding woman in her late fifties. Chambers had inherited the benefit of her protection from Abraham, whom Nora had also served for many years and it was impossible to get to Chambers without passing through Mrs Peach, who guarded him zealously. All new recruits to the firm were warned almost immediately that they crossed Mrs P at their peril.

Nonetheless on this early morning it was not Mrs Peach who had directed Chambers towards Stetchworth Station. At 6.15 he had been woken by his house phone, placed in his downstairs study in the house in Green Street which he shared with his Russian wife Nataly and their daughter Eugenia. The number was guarded carefully and was ex-directory to allow him some peace at home, so he answered the call expecting a friendly voice.

"Is that Mr Chambers?" asked a female voice.

"It is, who is speaking please?"

"It's Bridget Crehan, Mr Chambers," Chambers could hear the distress in her voice. He knew the name and presumed

19

she was the wife of Pat Crehan whom he had defended on a number of matters over previous years.

"What can I do for you Bridget?" Chambers asked, once more presuming that Pat had got into a bit of trouble with the police again.

"Pat's been arrested this morning. I wouldn't normally bother you Mr Chambers but I have a horrible notion that it is something to do with poor Tony."

"OK Bridget," Chambers' professional manner took over, "just slowly tell me what happened please."

Bridget took Chambers through the events of the morning as best she could. Her pulse was racing and she was imagining all kinds of unthinkable scenarios. At least the children were calm and had settled down very quickly. The police were still in the house and methodically bagging up all of Pat's clothing and shoes and they had asked her where Pat kept his gun. She had told them it was crazy to imagine that Pat had a gun. What did he need a gun for, for God's sake…

She ended by saying that they had taken Pat away in handcuffs and asking for his help.

Chambers reassured her as best he could. He promised her that he would leave for the police station as soon as he could and in any event within the next few minutes. He told her to make sure that she knew everything that the police took and made a list of all items as soon as they had left. He took her telephone number and promised to call her back once he had ascertained what was happening.

Bridget ended the phone call. She had done exactly what Pat had instructed her to do if ever he was arrested. She knew Chambers was by far the best solicitor in the town and the automatic choice of all criminals and people in trouble. But what had Pat done and why? The demons returned. As she tried to think through Pat's movements of the last few days since they had learned together of the shooting of Tony Blake and she could find nothing suspicious. Yes, he was often late to bed and she had invariably collapsed into a deep sleep well before midnight but there had been nothing noteworthy about Pat's behaviour for weeks. They both knew the Blakes. In truth Bridget did not much like them. She regarded Tony as an obvious bully but also felt that his wife knew and supported his behaviour. It was essential that Pat get along with Tony and perform well on any jobs that came his way from Tony's firm but she didn't consider the relationship between Pat and Tony as anything major and was always happy when Pat was able to secure work outside of what she considered the local mafia. She wondered what dreadful thing Tony must have done to provoke such a cold-blooded end. One thing at least that she was sure of was that her Pat could never do such a thing. Yes he had gone off the straight and narrow from time to time and yes, sometimes he appeared quite frightening from his demeanour. He was a big man, with longish hair and only one eye as the result of a teenage accident with some exploding slaked lime. Yes he mixed in questionable company from time to time and sometimes could not account for his movements when she had the temerity to ask where he had been, but she was happy to accept this in the usual give and take of a reasonably happy marriage, and this man who rolled on the floor with his little girls and showed much emotion during a sad film or someone else's hardship… this man could not possibly have anything to do with Tony Blake's shooting. She was sure of that.

There was a knock at the living room door and a policewoman appeared around the edge to advise her that they were now leaving and did she want them to do anything for her or the girls before they left?

Chambers pushed through the outside door of the Stetchworth Police Station at 7.20. He knew what to expect. He had already worked out that Crehan must have been implicated in the Blake murder. In musing over the likely suspects in the previous days neither Chambers nor his assistant solicitor and right-hand man Steve Evans had at any time considered Crehan as a real possibility. He was not in the same league of heavies as Blake and was more a petty criminal than a man of violence.

The look on the station sergeant's face told him that he was not expected. Crehan's request had been ignored in order to give those interrogating him time to make inroads before the undoubtedly unhelpful intervention of the lawyer they all knew and distrusted.

Chambers' arrival and request to see his client was most inconvenient. The desk sergeant knew that, as much as he might have wanted, and might have tried it on with a less experienced lawyer, he dare not deny that Crehan was in custody at the station in order to buy more time. In addition, this could well turn out to be a murder charge in due course and it was vital that no breaches of protocol took place that might later lead to challenges in the courts.

Chambers exchanged light-hearted pleasantries with the sergeant and after ten minutes was shown down to the holding cell where he came face to face with a dishevelled Crehan. He asked to be alone with his client and as soon as the cell door was shut gestured with his finger to his lips that Crehan was to say nothing.

He opened his solicitor's notebook, a hundred pages of lined script, each page with a perforated margin to allow easy extraction, and turned back the light blue cover. The first page carried simply the words in large capitals "CAN YOU READ?" At Crehan's rather bemused nod, Chambers turned to the second page where, similarly capitalized, he read "I WILL ASK THE QUESTIONS, JUST NOD OR SHAKE YOUR HEAD."

Crehan nodded.

"Is this arrest in connection with the Blake murder?" Crehan nodded again.

"Have they interviewed you yet?" He shook his head.

"Good. This is what will happen. I will tell them that you are not to be interviewed without my being present. If they try to interview you and make an excuse for my not being there, you are to refuse to answer any questions and must demand my presence. Understood?"

Crehan nodded.

"When I leave you, I will see what the senior officer is willing to tell me, and what they suspect you of. I don't want you to tell me anything at this stage. If they think you are simply a bit player I will discuss possible bail, but you should settle down for at least a 24 hour stay."

Chambers turned another page to the words, "WRITE DOWN THE NAME OF ANYONE I SHOULD CONTACT OR ANYTHING YOU MIGHT WANT DOING WHEN I LEAVE."

He handed the page to Crehan who thought for a moment before hurriedly scribbling, "AINT DONE NOTHING THIS IS A FIT UP."

Chambers looked him in the face and said "OK Pat, you've been here before. You know the score. I'll be back when they interview you. I've spoken to Bridget. She and the kids are alright.

"Remember," he continued, again putting his finger to his lips, "at all times with anyone, other than to ask for tea."

He grinned and patted Crehan on the arm reassuringly.

He pressed the buzzer at the door which was opened immediately, causing him to turn to his client with an "I told you so" look on his face, and he left Pat to study the wall.

So it had all begun. Chambers had found no senior officer available to discuss the case.

After two interviews at which Chambers had been present and at which no meaningful questions were asked or answered Crehan was formally charged with the murder of Tony Blake. He was refused police bail.

At 10.30 the following day he appeared before the Stetchworth Magistrates where the learned magistrates were advised that police investigations were proceeding, that there was a welter of circumstantial evidence already accrued against the defendant and that there were severe objections to bail for all of the usual reasons. Crehan was a violent criminal (aside from a youthful conviction for assault occasioning actual bodily harm – in this case a slap of a probation officer – Crehan had no violent past), Crehan was a flight risk (where was he going to go and desert his wife and two young children who all attended), Crehan might seek to intimidate witnesses (what frigging witnesses?). Moreover the senior investigating officer had already seen fit to charge him with the offence.

Crehan was remanded in custody for a further 14 days.

Outside the courtroom, Steve Evans explained to Bridget what was going on and how events would transpire. There might be further interviews of Pat, at which Chambers would be present. In fourteen days' time the Magistrates were likely to be called upon to commit Pat to trial at the Crown Court at which stage they would be obliged to submit to the defence team whatever evidence they intended to rely upon in due course. It would be supplied in deposition form and only then would they all have a chance to look at and analyse the evidence. It would be open to the magistrates Court to decide that no case had been made and that it should not proceed to trial, but this rarely occurred and it was not usually good practice to allow the prosecution in a case like this to rehearse their case before historically prosecution-minded magistrates who, being middle-class hangovers from Edwardian England, found it difficult to accept that police officers might occasionally tell lies.

By February Patrick Crehan had been committed to St Albans Crown Court to face the charge of murder. The depositions of the evidence upon which the prosecution intended to rely had been served upon the defence solicitors and Chambers and his team had commenced the detailed dissection of that evidence which of course involved regular trips to Jebb Avenue where dangerous prisoners were kept on remand pending trial.

And so, inexorably for Pat, time had passed and come to this moment. He was about to be represented by a Queen's Counsel whom he had not met until this morning. He had gone through several conferences with his solicitors and junior counsel Laurence Kerslake for whom he had huge respect. Kerslake had put the homework in and knew the case backwards. Chambers' team all knew the intricacies of the case. They had lived with it for a long time now and were incredibly supportive of him.

Unfortunately the QC who had been briefed on his behalf over a month ago had been stricken with a family tragedy and been forced to withdraw only a week ago which meant that Pat was now represented at the highest level by an alternative who had only taken the brief five days ago and first impressions were not favourable.

James Salpetre QC was of the old school of British families. He had been born into an aristocratic family, the eldest son, and had inherited the baronetcy on the untimely death of his father. He did not however allow himself to be referred to in chambers as Sir James and this outward demonstration of modesty had gone in his favour. However, educated at Eton and then Oxford, he could hardly pretend that he was not a son of privilege.

After Oxford he had worked on the family's Malaysian rubber plantation to give him a taste of the Orient and an idea of what graft had created the family fortune, from which he was destined to benefit.

He had returned to pupillage at 5 Kings Bench Walk and decided that he liked the cut and thrust of the daily battles in the courts that life as a criminal barrister provided. His career had flourished and today he found himself a highly successful criminal QC, a happily married father of three and a Tory MP for a safe seat in the Kentish countryside. He had taken the brief at short notice for several reasons. Lewis Semken his brilliant friend had been beset by personal misfortune and whilst there were other silks in his Chambers who would also have been willing to take on this difficult case, James felt it was incumbent upon himself to help out his friend at a time of need. Also he was unusually free for the three weeks that this case was scheduled for and, with his mind, there was nothing he could not get on top of at very short notice.

And so, at 9 am that morning, within minutes of the prisoners' transportation arriving at the Crown Court from Brixton, he found himself sitting opposite the disarming features of Pat Crehan with Geoffrey Chambers sitting alongside him. Salpetre was a big man himself, standing at six feet four and weighing in at 16 stone but Chambers was at least six foot two and an ex-rugby player and Pat Crehan must have hit the scales at about 13 stone and was a muscular six feet tall. Between them they seemed to fill the interview room. This was their first meeting although Salpetre and Chambers had been in several cases together where Chambers had been defending solicitor for one of the other defendants not represented by Salpetre. The silk had a healthy respect for the brain of the solicitor and that had been added to by the telephoned commendation of Lewis the night before, who had advised James that Geoffrey Chambers was both clean and intelligent. Clean in the sense that he would not be the sort to introduce for his client any kind of previously unthought of defence and clean in the sense that he was honest and incorruptible.

"I've read my brief thoroughly. You'll understand that I was only finally briefed last Friday due to Lewis' unfortunate problem but I assure you I have done nothing other than go through the depositions and sleep for the last 48 hours," he started after they had all exchanged some banter amidst formal introductions.

Scrutinizing Salpetre carefully with his one eye, Crehan tried to apply some objectivity to his situation. It had taken him some time to accept that Geoffrey was not going to be standing on his two feet with Pat sitting behind him alongside Steve and Feargal, the young clerk he had come to like and trust. Geoff was a solicitor and this was the Crown Court. It would be much more appropriate and sensible to have two barristers as the front team. They were experts in advocacy, the top of their trade. Pat was entitled under his Legal Aid to have Leading Counsel and it would be folly not to, as all had advised him. Over the past months he had grown to admire Lewis Semken for his grasp of the case and intelligence, but now, at the very last moment he was dealt this blow. The man opposite him could be forgiven his posh accent and overbearingly patrician manner, although Pat would not have described it in those words, but as this first encounter wore on he was receiving the distinct impression that Salpetre wanted to run the defence his way with a degree of give and take and with a pragmatic lawyer's approach to the evidence, letting in by way of agreed deposition matters that could not possibly harm the defence.

Crehan had never seen it this way. He was absolute in his denial of involvement in the crime in any way. It was clear from the depositions that there was no truthful evidence against him and so everything, however trivial, was to be questioned and opposed, regardless of significance. All of the evidence against him was circumstantial. It was the entirety of that evidence that might convince a clear thinking jury that there could be no smoke without fire and that the welter of evidence enabled them to convict him beyond reasonable doubt. He wanted to poke holes in that evidence at every opportunity however meaningless in the overall action.

Semken had been swung round to this, and had been surprised when the youngest member of the team, Feargal, undoubtedly with a bright future in front of him, but clearly not understanding that in the exalted legal presence he found himself in the first conference he was to be seen and not heard, had uttered with the confidence and precocity only youth carries, "It's a barrel of apples, isn't it? We need to show the rotting ones that corrupt the whole barrel."

Semken had looked at Chambers and Evans, the former had an eyebrow raised and the hint of a smile, the latter his head bowed and was clearly embarrassed at the interjection from the youngster who had yet to learn how things worked.

"Yes, quite so, quite so. Now let's get back to the Appletree statement…" Lewis had got the conference back to the business in hand, but he liked the simile and thought about using it when final speeches came around.

"First business today will be getting the jury sworn in," explained the Tory MP for Maidenbury.

All three men in the room knew that but forgave him for stating the obvious.

"How do we feel about jurors?'

"I want you to ask each of them individually if they think coppers tell lies," Crehan started.

"We have the dubious pleasure in being in front of Antrim-Davies. No doubt Mr Chambers has told you all about him. He will not let us attack jurors with such a question…"

27

Nigel Antrim-Davies was the resident Crown Court judge at St Albans and was notoriously pro the prosecution in all matters. Defence counsel dreaded being before him, both because it lessened markedly their chances of success but also because they did not relish the disdain with which the ageing judge treated them

"What do you suggest?" Pat asked.

Salpetre did not want to aggravate Antrim-Davies at the very outset of business and was himself very doubtful that this line would prove successful for Crehan. The British public in the early 70s were loath to espouse either conspiracy theories or that their friendly local policemen could be capable of telling lies. It was a common belief that the police would not charge someone unless he was guilty.

"I think we should stay quiet and if anything only challenge the elderly and obviously middle-class jurors. Younger men, especially black men are more likely to be suspicious of the police evidence."

"No, I can't be having that," Pat began. "This case has to be put the way I want it. The police are lying throughout as are all of the witnesses and we must try to put it to the jurors from the start."

"Well, let's consider that," the barrister countered. "We don't actually want to suggest that all of the evidence is lies, do we? A lot of it goes nowhere to implicating you and my view is we would be better to let it go through unchallenged as it does us no harm. If we suggest that everything is untrue then we will quickly appear paranoid to the jury and, more important, to old Antrim, who will put the knife in…"

Crehan was visibly agitated. This was not going the way he wanted. He had been stewing at Her Majesty's Pleasure for seven months now. During which he had had plenty of time to consider his position. Moreover, whilst on remand he had spent many hours in the company of men who had spent much of their lives fighting conviction and who had not been backwards in giving Pat their views on the reality of the system.

"I get what you're saying, but very little of the neutral evidence is actually neutral and it's important to me that this question is asked of the jurors. I also want you to ask them if they know any policemen…"

28

"Why do you want me to ask that?'

"Because if they have a friend who is a copper or their wife is friends with a copper's wife, they will have set views on criminals, and lawyers for that matter. They will have been given the usual bollocks about how the police never arrest someone without cause, how lawyers bend the truth and make up defences for their clients and so on. You know that…"

"Yes, I do, but we have to be tactical in our approach. My job is to get you off these charges and I will do my utmost to achieve that for you but you do need to let me conduct your case in the way that I deem best for you."

Chambers felt it was time to intervene.

"We can decide on our approach to all of the evidence as it progresses. There is no necessity to decide right now just how we are going to treat it. For instance, Pat, you may find that when she gives her evidence, Mrs Appletree is very favourable towards you in person whereas in her deposition she seems dead against you, in which case we might want to go softly with her and so on. But I do think James that it would not hurt to challenge the jurors as they are sworn in. At least it will give them the message…"

"Very well, let's see what we can get away with. Now," said Salpetre, pointedly looking at his watch, "we are due in in ten minutes and I have a couple of things I need to attend to first. I'll see you up there."

Once he had left the room, Crehan looked at Chambers and shook his head,

"I'm not keen, Geoffrey, you're going to have to keep tight on him. He thinks he's running my case, he's got another think coming."

"Ok, Pat, keep your cool for now, let's see how the morning proceeds…

As you enter Court One at St Albans from the public end, the public gallery is on your right, with five rows of seats either side of a gangway giving seating for about 80 people. Ahead is the jury box down the left-hand wall. To the far-right corner just in front of the judge's bench is the witness box. Below the raised dais upon which the judge's chair is placed in front of the Royal Coat of Arms emblazoned in relief on the far white wall, are the desks of the various court officials, the judge's clerk, the court ushers, the stenographer and others. Next away from them are the benches and chairs housing the prosecution team of Edward Ableman Q.C. and his junior counsel Brian Toynbee, their instructing solicitors from the Crown Prosecution service and one or two assistants. Adjacent to the jurybox side of them were seated Salpetre and behind him Kerslake. Behind him were Chambers and Evans and behind them was young Feargal, uncomfortable in the new pinstriped navy suit that Chambers had insisted he go and buy the previous weekend.

Behind them in the dock sat Pat Crehan flanked by two officers. Crehan had already established a relationship with his accompanying guard. They both knew from experience that it was best to be on good terms with an unconvicted prisoner. It would lead to a much easier three or four weeks on the arduous journey to and from court for all of them and besides any defendant in a murder trial, particularly one such as this where he was seriously protesting his innocence, was sure to find the whole experience extremely stressful.

Chambers and then Evans had both remained with Crehan during the previous ten minutes in order to keep him calm and let him know that everyone was working for him. They had only resumed their seats when a court clerk had indicated to them that the judge was about to begin.

There was a loud knock.

"All rise," announced an usher and everyone in the courtroom rose to their feet.

His Honour Judge Nigel Antrim-Davies entered the court from the door that led to the back corridor linking the courtroom to his chambers. He was a fairly slight individual, dressed in the customary wig and red gown of a Crown Court judge with tight half-moon clear framed spectacles perched on the end of an aquiline nose.

He took his seat and peered over the edge of his spectacles at the courtroom before him and took in the scene before adjusting his view down to his clerk directly below him.

"Yes, Mrs James?"

She nodded back at him.

"Defendant please stand."

Pat had not sat down and had his hands resting on the polished mahogany at the front of the dock.

"Are you Patrick Anthony Crehan?' she asked.

"I am Your Honour" said Pat in a firm voice

"Patrick Anthony Crehan, you are charged that on or around November 6th 1972 you did murder Tony Richard Blake at Grace Road in Stetchworth, Hertfordshire. Do you plead guilty or not guilty to the charge?"

"Not guilty"

"You may be seated."

Antrim-Davies raised his eyes towards the assembled barristers who responded by rising to their feet and the two Queen's Counsel introduced themselves and their juniors formally.

"Let's proceed with the jury…"

Feargal witnessed the various proposed jury members filing in. He was no newcomer to the court. He had been working for Geoffrey since the previous September. His relationship with the law firm had started several years ago. He was a talented pupil at the local grammar school. Top in his class and a competent sportsman, Feargal had been popular with classmates and enjoyed his school life considerably. He was the son of a Stetchworth primary school headmaster who had come to the town in the mid-1950s to take up a headship at a new school as part of the New Towns experiment. Stetchworth had been a wonderful place to grow up. The family home was on the verge of a huge playing field which was home to countless football pitches and several cricket fields. Freedom for the local children was unbounded and there was a sense that everyone knew each other and were involved in some common venture. There was a great sense of community and belonging and children thrived.

As a 14-year-old Feargal had been encouraged to start to think about careers. Despite his love of animals his school results had dictated that he should look away from the sciences side of study when looking for a future. He had alighted upon a career in law, encouraged by his Careers Master at the school. The school ran a Works Experience Week and arranged for the boys to take a week out from their studies and go and work in the local factories and businesses to get a feel for what the everyday work in their chosen careers involved. The budding engineers would go to British Aircraft Corporation or George W King or one of the other many engineering-related companies that had flocked to Stetchworth in the 50s. Would-be teachers went to other schools in the area. And so, aided by an inventive placement officer in the form of the careers master, the school was rid of most of its 14-year-olds for a week. How many returned with a firmer idea of what they wanted to do in life was anyone's guess.

Feargal however had been sent to work with Geoffrey Chambers for a week and from that week onwards he did not contemplate any other career.

Chambers was fun to be with but he demanded total dedication from his staff. The atmosphere in the huge offices which spread over the top of the Stetchworth General Post Offices was one of dedicated professionalism and teamwork, from the cleaners through the secretaries and administrative staff, through the Legal Executives and Articled Clerks then up again through the solicitors of different age and experience to the Partners themselves. Chambers ran the office with a light touch. All of his staff could and did approach him on varied subjects both legal and otherwise, and the young men in the office, far from being intimidated by him, enjoyed sharing with him their successes and failures their worries and hopes, safe in the knowledge that he was of huge good humour and treated them all as his personal wards.

Feargal had never experienced anything like it and was fascinated. Always treated seriously and with respect by Chambers and his staff, by the end of the week he had visited at least ten different Magistrates Courts where Chambers had numerous cases. He had been to a Crown Court and sat with Chambers whilst the barrister delivered a plea in mitigation for a guilty defendant. The same barrister had then taken them to a lunch afterwards. Feargal had never been to a restaurant for lunch. Moreover he was enthused, and sure that he had discovered the career that he wished to pursue.

Twelve jurors had taken their seats. Ten men and two women. Each now had to stand and take an oath on the Bible to try the matter before them honestly and in good faith. The first juror was handed the Bible by the court usher and asked to stand. As he did so Salpetre rose to his feet and it seemed that the whole courtroom bristled.

"Your Honour, as you are aware I represent the defendant, Mr Crehan, in this matter."

Antrim-Davies nodded and peered over his half-glasses. He sensed trouble ahead.

"Yes Mr Salpetre…?"

"Your Honour, it is my instruction to put to each member of the jury a certain question. It will depend on the answer given to that question whether the defence will challenge the empanelling of that juror'

"Well, Mr Salpetre, this should have been raised before the jury was brought in. I think I must ask the jury to retire before I consider whether to allow the question to be put."

"Very well, Your Honour," started Salpetre. "I apologise for the inconvenience."

Antrim-Davies nodded a grudging smile and beckoned to the usher who then led out the jury.

Once the jury had all been led out, the judge peered at Salpetre.

"Now, Mr Salpetre what is this particular question?"

Salpetre rose to his feet.

"Your Honour, my instructions are to ask each individual juror the question as follows: 'Do you believe that members of the police force are capable of lying in court?'"

It was immediately apparent from his demeanour and the following words that Antrim-Davies was never going to allow such a question.

"Before I rule on this I will of course wish to hear what Leading Counsel for the prosecution has to say on this matter but I must advise, Mr Salpetre, that I am disinclined in the extreme to allow such a question. Of course I acknowledge that your client's defence may well be that a number of police officers giving evidence in this case, and I have read all of the depositions, are lying. However it is for the jury to hear and weigh the evidence on the basis that each and every witness, all of whom will have sworn the testamentary oath, may or may not be lying. Their individual predisposition to this or any other belief is, in my view, irrelevant to these proceedings... Mr Ableman?"

Ableman rose and agreed with the judge, adding that he had never in his entire career encountered a situation where a question such as that proposed had been allowed. He sat down promptly, not wishing to incur the legendary wrath of Antrim-Davies for telling him what he already knew.

In the dock, Crehan's agitation was apparent and becoming more vocal. First Feargal and then Steve had been beckoned to him and various notes passed up to counsel.

Salpetre rose. He could not defy his client's repeated instruction to further press the judge to allow the question yet inwardly he felt it was impossible to succeed in anything other than setting the irascible judge against them from the outset.

"Your Honour," he began, "I fully understand Your Honour's inclination and take on board the comments of my learned friend, however this is an exceptional case. It relies entirely on circumstantial evidence, most of which will be delivered by police officers. My client has been present before this court previously as a defendant and acquitted of the charges against him when the police officers were found to have fabricated their evidence. Your Honour will appreciate that it is therefore most important to the defendant that the open-mindedness of the jury is established as a precondition of them hearing the case.."

The judge nodded and began again.

"I have heard what counsel for the defendant has submitted. I will not allow this question to be put to the jurors. Mr Salpetre, would you like 15 minutes to consult with your client?"

"I would Your Honour."

"Very well, we will resume at 11.45 when the jury may be brought back in."

It was agreed with the accompanying officers that rather than Pat be taken below, he would stay in the dock and the impromptu conference take place there

"Well, no success there, but we made our point," began Salpetre trying to inject early optimism into the discussion.

"The old cunt wasn't ever going to allow it," Pat began. "Now what do we do about these jurors?"

Laurence Kerslake decided he could now be useful. It was frustrating for a talented junior sitting behind a QC. The most one could expect was a few bits of minor cross examination and the introduction of the uncontroversial evidence for the defence. However, he reasoned he was being as well paid as the Legal Aid system would allow and he felt at one with the Chambers defence team.

"Let's analyse what kind of jury we want." He started, "My strong feeling is that we want the sort of person who can contemplate officers lying through their teeth and anyone who might have suffered at their hands… I was hoping for a black guy or two but there were none in the original 12 and I did not see any of the reserves. Let's post Feargal outside court and he can report in on the make-up of the six or so reserves left outside court. I think we should challenge anyone over 60 and any female over 30. All the studies I have read show that the faith in the police force is strongest in those groups…"

Chambers looked at Pat inquiringly.

"Yes, I will let you know who to challenge, "

The barristers returned to their positions and indicated that they were ready to resume when it suited the usher. Crehan, meanwhile, grabbed Chambers by the arm and kept him by the edge of the dock.

"He's no fucking good, Geoffrey, I think we'd be better off without him…"

"Give him time," said Chambers. "Look if we sack him we don't know who else we can get at short notice. Laurence can't do it for professional reasons… if you sack the Leader, the junior goes too, and as much as Laurence is with us, he will not break protocol on this one."

"Ha, I'm the one that's going to get time, Geoffrey, if we don't do something. One more ricket and he's going. I'll do it myself."

Chambers flashed him a quizzical look and tried to calm him down. "Let's concentrate on getting the best jury we can and then I think Antrim will adjourn for lunch. Talking of which, are you sorted for food?"

"No, I'm alright, the wife's already left some lunch down there for me."

The selection of the jurors was not without incident. The first juror to stand up to take the oath was immediately met by a loud "No! Challenge" from the dock and the unfortunate recipient was asked respectfully by Antrim-Davies to follow the usher back outside and await further direction. Before that, Feargal had entered court to report on the composition of the reserves waiting outside, news that was not particularly supportive of Laurence's suggested plan. In any event, four challenges later the jury of 12 was finally sworn in and as predicted, the judge had proposed an early lunch adjournment.

Feargal was despatched to buy some sandwiches for the team, Salpetre wanted to work on the evidence proposed for the afternoon and Kerslake had accompanied him.

Geoffrey and Stephen were left alone together in their seats.

"I think he is going to erupt this afternoon," Stephen started.

"Yes, he wants to challenge absolutely everything. He sees a conspiracy against him in everything. I think our role is to make sure he at least has some representation by the end of the day. I suspect he will go haywire with nobody left to support him," Chambers agreed and then continued, "I can see his point, but we haven't even started yet. Old Antrim will wind him up. What we do not want is for the jury to regard him as a loony with a scattergun defence. We have got to help him concentrate on the main targets. Mrs Appletree is a good example. We don't want him launching into her for no reason on day one."

"I agree," said Stephen, " but I can guarantee that Salpetre will want to take it very softly with her and Pat won't want that approach."

Chambers nodded and grimaced. They would soon find out.

Feargal returned with the sandwiches.

At ten minutes before two o'clock the sound of voices below the dock preceded the return of the defendant. He was exchanging some joke or other with the officer with him concerning the trip back that evening to Brixton. As his face appeared he immediately beckoned Geoffrey over.

"Were you fed ok?' asked Chambers

"Oh yes, they let B bring me in a packed lunch each day. They are very good with you whilst you are on remand. It's different if you're convicted. I've been thinking about this brief. I think I'd rather have you than him defend me."

"I can't Pat. Solicitors have no right of audience in the Crown Court. They may have one day but for the time being I cannot. We can ask for an adjournment to appoint a fresh counsel but it could set you back many weeks and we still may not get one you like. Please give him a bit longer. If you still insist on a change tonight we can discuss it then."

"The damage could be done by then."

There were brief opening addresses to the jury by both silks. Ableman played up the horrific and cold-blooded nature of the killing. As would be expected, he laboured, nobody actually saw the killer pull the trigger and therefore the entirety of the evidence against Crehan was circumstantial. It would be like piecing a jigsaw together but eventually the overwhelming conclusion formed from all of the pieces of evidence would be that on the night of November 5th it had been Patrick Crehan who had lain in wait for the victim, and shotgunned him to death.

Salpetre took a simple approach. The killing had been brutal. The accused and the victim knew each other. There was no evidence of bad blood between them. There was simply no compelling evidence that would lead a jury to convict Crehan on the basis that it had been proved beyond reasonable doubt that Crehan had committed the crime. It was not his client's duty to prove who had committed the murder, that was a job for the police, who as would be demonstrated had fallen a long way short of proving their case here.

"Thank you Mr Salpetre," began Antrim-Davies once Salpetre had sat down. "Mr Ableman, would you like to call your first witness?'

"Indeed Your Honour, Mrs Emily Appletree please."

A few minutes later preceded by the court usher, a frail elderly lady moved slowly into the witness box.

Emily Appletree was now 68 and had not aged well. She had been born in the east of London's docklands. Her great grandparents had fled to London during the late nineteenth century where her great grandfather like his son after him and his son after him found work in the docks. Emily and her husband had seized the opportunity of escaping to Stetchworth at the invitation of the local development council who were busy clearing the old East End to make way for new offices and shops in the post war clearance. A comfortable council house in Stetchworth and the promise of an abundance of jobs for Bill had sealed the deal and they had found themselves quickly on a removal truck and heading up the A1. They had been there since 1959 and considered themselves Stetchworth locals now.

Emily lived on the corner of the internal group of houses that made up Elm Square. The Square had houses all around the perimeter and where there would have been green space in the middle of a London Square, here there was another block of houses all of which faced outwards to the road between the inner square and the outer houses and whose gardens adjoined each other at the rear. A small pathway gave access to the rear gate of each garden.

"Now, Mrs Appletree, you live at 59 Elm Square in Stetchworth. Is that correct?"

"Yes it is."

"And how long have you lived there?"

"For the last 13 years"

"And would it be true to say that you know most of your immediate neighbours?'

"Yes."

"Now do you recognize the man facing you in the dock?" Ableman gestured towards Pat Crehan.

"Yes I do, that is Mr Crehan who lives at 72."

"Let me take you back to the early hours of November 6th. Can you tell the court what you saw?"

Crehan was getting agitated in the dock. He summoned Feargal over but Chambers heard him and went to the dock himself.

"What's the matter."

"He needs to stop this old bag."

"She's not being led. He'll be able to cross examine her and anyway, she doesn't do you any harm…"

"She's fucking lying"

"Calm down, let him do his job"

Crehan shook his head and exhaled loudly as Chambers returned.

"Yes, I was looking out into the street at about 2.15 when I saw a man in a long black coat and holding something walk down the other side of the street and disappear into the passageway that leads to Mr Crehan's house."

"And did you recognize that it was Mr Crehan?"

"I was fairly sure it was him."

"Why do you say that you were fairly sure?"

"Well, it was dark but the man looked as though he was Mr Crehan and had similar length hair."

"Thank you Mrs Appletree. Please remain there as I am sure my friend will wish to ask you a few questions."

Salpetre rose slowly to his feet. He wanted to tread very gently and adopted his long practiced best avuncular manner.

"Mrs Appletree, thank you. Tell us, please, why were you looking out into the street at 2.15 in the morning? Most of us are fast asleep then…" He smiled, aware that the jurors were probably thinking the very same.

"My sciatica was playing up so I had gone downstairs for a cup of tea."

"I see and presumably you had put on the lights in your kitchen?"

"Yes, my kitchen faces the road"

"And are there curtains over the windows?"

"Yes. I looked out because I heard a noise"

"I see. And what kind of noise did you hear?"

"I'm not sure what it was"

"And that's when you saw a figure on the street?'

"Yes"

"The street lights were off by this time, weren't they?"

"Yes."

"But looking out behind your curtains, with your kitchen light on you made out a man 30 yards away?"

"Yes."

"And you thought it might be Mr Crehan?"

"Well it looked like him and went into his house"

"Yes, you've been very fair and thank you for that, but you could not be sure it was the defendant, could you?"

"No, not a hundred per cent."

"Thank you. Now tell me, when were you first asked about this. Because I presume seeing a black coated figure that you did not recognize in the street was something you would probably forget about fairly quickly, isn't it?"

"The police officer came and asked me if I could remember anything about that night about five days later"

"And did the officer ask you if you had seen Mr Crehan that night?"

"Yes."

"Tell me, how bad is your sciatica?"

"Oh , it's chronic. I'm up most nights with it."

"And are you absolutely sure that it was on the night of November 5th that you were up and saw the figure in the road?"

"Yes"

"It couldn't have been the 4th or the 6th?"

"No, I'm sure."

"But you were probably up with the dreaded sciatica on those nights too?"

"I can't remember now."

"Did the officer remind you that the night was the 5th?"

"She said that was the night she was interested in."

"Thank you Mrs Appletree, that's most helpful."

Salpetre sat down, sure he had achieved as much as he could hope for. His closing speech would be the time to remind the jury of the questionable nature of the old lady's evidence.

Ableman decided not to re-examine. He knew what ground Salpetre had gained and did not want to push his luck in case his re-examination opened up more gaps.

What happened next was a surprise to all in the courtroom save the defendant who was on his feet and had his hand raised in the air.

"Mr Salpetre," Antrim-Davies who had of course seen the defendant's actions from his seat, addressed the learned counsel for the Defence, "Your client…"

Salpetre glanced around behind him and saw the glowering countenance of Crehan. He raised his eyebrows and indicated to Chambers that he should find out what was the problem.

Geoffrey Chambers was not easily embarrassed. As he headed back towards his client however, he realized that what he was about to hear and therefore what he was about to have to do was going to embarrass him considerably.

"Get rid of him, Geoffrey," were the words that Crehan greeted him with.

Geoff discussed the matter in as far as he could with the irate client he did not want to lose. He explained that Salpetre had done a good job in his cross examination of Mrs Appletree and that when they returned to the evidence he would make tons of capital out of it. Pat Crehan did not see it that way however. He was under intense pressure as are all defendants and perhaps his powers of reason were not quite as good as they should have been. He was adamant he had not been in the Square that night and his wife would be giving evidence that he had been at home all night. Thus Mrs Appletree was lying and, in Crehan's view, should have been confronted with her lie and the suggestion that the policewoman who had interviewed her had put words into her mouth should also have been put directly. There was no reasoning with Crehan and eventually, in full view of the court and the jury, Chambers was forced to return to the Queen's Counsel and his junior and explain to them that they had a serious difficulty and that an adjournment would be necessary.

Antrim-Davies had a fair idea of what was transpiring.

"Mr Salpetre, would it be appropriate to adjourn proceedings for the day? We are getting towards that time anyway?"

Salpetre rose and nodded and Antrim-Davies embarked on warning the jury under no circumstances to discuss the case with anyone and to report again for duty the following day at 9.30.

"All rise!" barked the clerk as the judge took his leave and within two minutes the only people left in the courtroom were the two sets of barristers and the entire defence team, minus their client who had been taken down to the holding cells.

"Oh dear, silly man," was the muted response from Salpetre after Chambers had explained the position. "I'd better explain to Ableman. Is he likely to reconsider his position overnight? Antrim will not be amused."

Laurence was visibly disappointed, "Bloody idiot. He's got every chance in this with this sort of evidence but on his own…?" he grimaced.

Chambers and the barristers discussed the correct court etiquette and it was decided that, having advised Ableman of the situation, Salpetre and Ableman would approach the judge in person and advise that both defence barristers would be discontinuing and would not be replaced.

Crehan was set on defending himself.

And so day two began of the Crehan murder trial, so- called.
But the whole atmosphere within Court One at St Albans had
changed. It was black and white, us and them, lies and falsehood.

Antrim-Davies explained to the jury that the Defendant had
decided to dispense with the services of counsel. He would for
the remainder of the trial be defending himself with the aid of his
solicitors whom he had retained. No inference was to be made of
the evidence to date and all future proceedings would be conducted
in the same manner notwithstanding this unusual turn of events.

The judge then addressed Crehan and advised him that he
respected his decision and that he would grant him a certain
degree of latitude due to his layman status but that nonetheless,
he, the judge, was in charge of this trial and that Crehan was to
appreciate that at all times.

Most of the evidence produced on day two was non-contentious.
The forensic officer who had examined the body confirmed that the
victim had died from multiple traumas occasioned by two blasts
from what appeared to have been a 12-bore shotgun. Photographs
were shown to the jury before lunch of Tony Blake's upper body,
front and back, peppered with pellet wounds. The gunman,
whoever it was had done a highly competent job. Nobody could
have survived one blast, let alone two.

The same highly experienced Home Office forensic expert
produced after lunch a number of other exhibits that he had
been asked to examine.

One was a shotgun.

"Mr Dufficy, the court officer will now produce to you Exhibit
23 in this case" commenced Ableman, and the dismantled shotgun,
broken into its constituent parts and wrapped in polythene and
labelled was handed to the man in the witness box.

"Would you kindly take out and assemble the exhibit, Mr
Dufficy?"

Dufficy withdrew the handle, barrels and stock and very
quickly had the complete shotgun in his arms. He held it in
one hand facing the ceiling of the courtroom and looked back
at his questioner.

"Thank you," continued Ableman "Now I believe you have seen and examined this exhibit before. Please advise the court what you know about it…"

"This is the 12-gauge shotgun which the police brought to me. I was advised that they had strong suspicions that it was the same weapon that was used in this murder."

"And have you been able to verify whether this was or was not the murder weapon?"

"No, I have not."

"Could you please tell the court why?"

"Yes. Put simply, shotguns are not like other guns and rifles. When the cartridge is exploded out of the barrel, literally hundreds of pellets are expelled towards the target which fan out on their own separate trajectories until they hit something. Because of this they carry no identifier of the barrel from which they come, whilst the singularity of a bullet ensures that as it travels down the barrel it rotates and carries the unmistakeable fingerprint of the barrel down which it has travelled." He paused and took a sip of water anticipating further questioning

"In your opinion could this have been the murder weapon?"

"Yes, I believe it could have been. I carried out numerous tests on this shotgun and my conclusion is that it is possible, given the spread and range of discharge that this weapon could possibly be the murder weapon."

"And did you carry out any further examinations?"

"Yes, I carried out a full examination for fingerprints. The only fingerprints found on the weapon were from a control sample I had been given by the police prior to my examination, which I believe belonged to one of the young boys who found the weapon."

"Thank you, Mr Dufficy. Now I would like you to inspect Exhibit 27. Would the court officer please show the witness Exhibit 27."

The court officer brought over to the witness a large dark black coat.

"Do you recall this coat?'

"Yes, this is a coat labelled as taken from the home of the defendant on November 6th last year."

"Were you asked to examine the coat for traces of gunshot discharge residue?"

At this Chambers who was seated directly in front of Crehan turned to his client and mouthed some instructions. Crehan stood up and shouted "Objection."

Surprisingly he received quick help from the judge,

"Yes Mr Ableman, you know very well that you cannot lead the witness on matters as sensitive as this. Moreover the court needs your help in a case like this where the defendant does not have full representation to act properly and fairly. Now should we start again?"

"I beg your pardon Your Honour. Mr Dufficy, when you examined Exhibit 27 what exactly did you find?"

Dufficy resumed. "I found small monoxide traces consistent with those caused by shotgun discharge around the area of the right waist pocket of the coat."

"Thank you, Mr Dufficy. Please wait there."

Crehan stood up. He had been properly briefed and soon had Dufficy admit that if the coat had been close to the discharge of an exhaust pipe from a car, he may have found the same result. He also conceded that he had no way of accurately assessing when the deposit had been made.

Crehan continued. "Now I want you to think very hard before answering my next question, Mr Dufficy. You are telling the court that this weapon may have been the one that killed the deceased, but you cannot be sure. Is that correct?'

"Yes."

"Do you have within your knowledge the number of 12-bore shotguns in existence in this country alone?"

Ableman began to rise to object, but the judge intervened.

"Do you by chance know the statistic, Mr Dufficy?"

"I believe the number exceeds 75,000 Your Honour."

"Thank you."

Crehan began again, "And can we assume that you ran extensive forensic checks on this coat for any other thing unusual upon it?"

"I did."

"And you found nothing else of note?"

"Nothing whatsoever."

As he left the courtroom Dufficy could have no idea how his evidence was yet to figure largely later in the trial.

Chambers and his team spent a torrid hour down in the cells with Crehan. He had performed calmly and methodically with Dufficy who had been the epitome of fairness. Chambers stressed again how it was imperative to be calm, even when the answers from the witnesses were not what Pat wanted. All of them knew that the heavy evidence was starting in the morning and would set the tone for the jury.

Crehan eventually departed into the prison bus and a pensive defence team made their respective ways home. All of them lived in Stetchworth save for Steve Evans who lived with his girlfriend Jane in a Hertfordshire village nearer to St Albans. They were all tense and glad to retreat to their respective domestic situations, Chambers to his wife and daughter in Stetchworth Old Town and Feargal to his mum's cooking, for he still lived at home in a leafy area of the town.

Day three began without any external drama. The team were beginning to settle into a steady routine. Feargal would join Geoffrey in the office shortly after 7.30 am with Mrs Peach and go through the numerous other cases that had come through the doors of the firm in the last few days. Never had the boy faced such responsibility as Chambers threw case after case at him as he barked instructions to require details from the defendants where they were on bail, get phone numbers of proposed witnesses, contact case officers, double check facts and so on. Mrs Peach looked at Chambers disapprovingly. Didn't he realise this was a green young man, fresh out of school with no experience of the world beyond A Levels and certainly not the world he had been plunged into?

Chambers looked up and could see what she was thinking.

"Nora, don't worry. He's a very capable young man and if he is struggling with anything he can ask you, won't you Fearg?"

The boy smiled with a confidence beyond his years, "Don't worry Mrs P., I won't let the side down and if I do I'll blame it on you anyway!"

She tutted and blushed. She liked him but he was a different generation, and far too cocky.

Eventually they debunked and jumped into Chambers' Vitesse to get to court.

"You want me to instruct counsel on the three Hatfield cases?"

"Yes," replied the lawyer somewhat taken aback that the boy was ahead of him in the process, "I'll never have time to do these, ask Kings Bench Walk to give them to three juniors, we owe them some work. Ask Crabbers to do the briefs, he's got time to cope"

Crabbers was Robert Crabtree another assistant solicitor at the firm, indulging, to everyone's knowledge at the firm, save he was unaware of it, in an extramarital affair with one of the conveyancing solicitors at the Welwyn branch of the firm. Fortunately her husband was one of the few that were not aware of it. It had made Robert slightly unpopular at the firm... he had still not quite realized why... and he was peeved that he had not been asked to assist in the Crehan case and particularly irritated that a bright schoolboy was being preferred by the boss.

Conversation switched to the day ahead. It was going to be interesting. The most damning evidence proposed by the prosecution was going to come from a 32-year-old heroin addict, a man with no work history and a string of petty crime convictions. He was on the methadone programme and completely dependent on his weekly supply of the liquid from the pharmacy. It was a fact but nonetheless hard to believe.

Having been called, John Graham shuffled to the witness box led by the court usher. He was a tall man, well over six feet tall and appeared surprisingly to be fairly alert. He was sworn in and Ableman embarked on the task of extracting his evidence without leading him, a task he had long been dreading.

Having elicited his name and address Ableman proceeded, "Thank you, Mr Graham. Now would you identify the man sitting in the dock."

"Yes, it's Pat Crehan"

"And how long have you known Mr Crehan?'

"About five years."

"And how did you get to know him?"

"I first met him at the Billiard Hall."

"And what was he doing there?"

"Playing snooker"

Ableman hated this part of the job with a laconic witness. He wished he could lead him to the important evidence but he could feel the eagle eyes of the judge boring into him.

"Did you become friends?"

"I wouldn't say that but he would sometimes after that get me to do a few errands for him."

"Please tell the court, Mr Graham, what kind of errands?"

"Oh, you know, fetching ciggies for him and his friends, things like that."

"And you got to know him better over time?"

"Yes, I think he thought I was ok because I knew a lot of people around and didn't let him down."

"I see, and did he ask you to do something particular for him last October which surprised you?"

"Yeah, he asked me if I knew anyone who could get hold of a shooter for him."

"And what did you understand him to mean by a 'shooter'?"

"You know, a gun or a shotgun."

"And how did you reply?"

"I told him maybe I could but it would cost."

"And what did he say to this?"

"He said there was money in it for me if I could arrange it."

"And did you?"

"Yeah."

"Please tell the court how you did this."

Whilst this tortuous pulling out of information had been taking place, Crehan had been slowly becoming more and more obviously irritated. His sighs became increasingly more audible and any jury member glancing in his direction would have witnessed grimaces and gesticulations that only grew worse with the evidence. Chambers too was aware of what was happening and had by now moved to the dock to urge Crehan to show some restraint. He knew that theatricals from the dock rarely cut much ice with either judge or jury.

"I knew that my friend Ray Johnson knew a bloke over at Ware that could get hold of weapons and ammo so I had a word with him and asked him to see what he could do."

"And what transpired?"

"Come again?"

"What did happen, Mr Graham?"

"I saw Ray later that day and told him. He came back to me about a week later and said the bloke in Ware had a shotgun and cartridges and would let Ray have it for two hundred quid, no questions asked."

"Please continue. What happened next? I presume you advised the defendant?"

"I saw Pat the next day and he asked me to get it. I told him that of course I didn't have any money and he would have to bung me to pay Ray."

"And did he give you the money?"

"Yeah, I was doing some painting job for him anyway and he put the extra in my wages that week."

"And what happened after that?"

"Well Ray had no money neither and so I gave him the money for the gun and some time later he came round my flat one night and said he had it in a sack. He gave it to me and the next Saturday I went and met Pat and handed him the sack."

"Did you look at what was in the sack?"

"No, I don't like guns and anyway I knew what it was."

"So you just handed a sack of contents to the defendant?"

"Yeah."

"And when was this?"

"Like I said, I called Pat and met him in his Transit on the Saturday and handed it over."

"And where did you meet him for this handover?"

"He told me he would be parked in Bedwell Crescent opposite the shops at 10.30."

"And was that where you met?"

"Yes."

"And did you see the defendant at any time after that?"

"No, next thing I heard was Tony had been shotgunned and then that Pat had been nicked."

"Now I want to take you a time some weeks later when you found yourself in the cells at Stetchworth Police Station."

"Yeah."

"So why were you there?"

"I'd been hauled in after the murder."

"Well, we appreciate that Mr Graham, but there must have been a serious reason why you were arrested and placed in the police cells…?"

"The Pigs came to my house late on the Sunday night, told me I was wanted for questioning in the Tony Blake murder and rushed me into a police car. I was immediately taken to the cells, having been told I was nicked and the door slammed shut."

"So, just to be clear, you are alleging that you were neither cautioned nor charged before being placed in the cells?'

"Yeah, that's right"

"Well, surely Mr Graham, you have been arrested before and know your rights; didn't this strike you as a little odd?"

"Yeah, but it seemed they were all in a panic over the murder and I guessed it would all straighten itself out later."

"In any event, did you become aware that you were not alone in the cells?"

"Yeah, I heard the defendant shout out asking who the fuck was in the cells."

"And did you identify yourself?"

"Yeah, I knew it was the defendant and I asked him what was going on."

"He shouted it was bullshit and to keep my mouth shut."

"And what did you say?"

"Something along the lines of 'What the fuck have you got us in to?'"

"And did he reply?"

"I think he told me just to shut my mouth."

"Did he say anything else?"

"I can't remember."

"Thank you Mr Graham, please wait there…"

The judge looked down his spectacles at Crehan,

"Mr Crehan, would you like five minutes to consult with those advising you before you commence your examination of this witness?"

"Thank you Your Honour," Pat was learning the ropes quickly, "but I am ready to proceed."

He stared at Graham and paused before beginning in a measured tone, "How long have you been a heroin addict?"

"I'm not a heroin addict, I'm on the methadone programme."

"Methadone is a substitute used in the treatment of heroin addicts, isn't it?"

"If you say so."

Ableman rose to his feet, sensing trouble. He knew this could quickly get out of hand.

"Your Honour…"

"Yes Mr Ableman, I thought you might want to say something to me. Should we clear the court?"

Ableman was nodding.

"Ladies and gentlemen of the jury, this will I anticipate happen from time to time during this case. A legal point requires to be discussed between myself, the defendant and Mr Ableman who represents the Crown. It cannot be discussed openly in front of you and therefore I must ask you to retire for a short period to your jury room. The usher will direct you there and stay with you until it is time to return. I thank you for your patience."

Once the jury had filed out, Ableman rose in anticipation.

"Well Mr Ableman, what would you like to say?"

"Your Honour, it is fair to say that the Crown does not dispute that the witness is a heroin stroke methadone addict of many years with a string of drug-related convictions against his name. Nonetheless it will be for the jury to decide in due course just how much weight to attach to his evidence both from the evidence itself and its substantiation from other witnesses and from his demeanour. I wonder, given the now rather unique circumstances of the case whether we may proceed on the basis that before the defendant continues his cross examination that I disclose that the Crown concedes that the witness is both an addict and has multiple convictions?"

"What would you like to say on this, Mr Crehan?" the Judge looked at him and asked.

"First of all, Your Honour, I'm amazed that the prosecution have completed their examination of the witness and at no stage have they been honest enough with the jury to tell them that the witness is a criminal with multiple convictions and is a known heroin addict and notorious for it in Stetchworth!"

"I suspect, Mr Crehan, that the reason Mr Ableman did not introduce the fact of Mr Graham's numerous convictions was because he wanted to give you the opportunity to consider whether to introduce the same yourself in cross examination and because he knew your advisers would have cautioned you of the consequences of so doing…"

"Yes, I understand that. But I am on trial for murder here. It's irrelevant that I have previous. The fact is that the jury should know what kinds of people are giving evidence against me. For instance, why wasn't the jury told that this man is a paid police informant?"

The judge turned quizzically towards the Queens Counsel leading the prosecution case who had his head turned away in what seemed to be rather flustered conversation with the solicitor immediately behind him who then turned quickly to the case officer advising her.

"Mr Ableman?"

"Thank you, Your Honour. My instructions are that this allegation made by the defendant is untrue. The witness is not a police informant"

"Is it not possible," continued Antrim-Davies, "that the witness has been a police informant at times during his criminal career but beyond the actual knowledge of those instructing you?"

Ableman continued his discussions with those behind him before again addressing the judge,

"Your Honour, it remains my instructions that Mr Graham has never been and is not a known police informant."

The judge pursed his lips visibly.

"Very well. Mr Crehan, you have heard what Leading Counsel for the prosecution has said. You must make of it as you will. We will now recall the jury and you shall continue with your cross examination of the witness."

The judge nodded at the court usher and a few minutes later the jury were once again in their seats.

Crehan resumed with barely concealed aggression.

"So you've been a heroin addict for a number of years and you have numerous criminal convictions?"

"I have a few convictions and yes I do have a drugs history."

"Thank you for finally admitting this. So you do not actually know what was in the sack that you say you gave to me?"

"Yes, I know it was a shooter"

"But you have no idea what kind of gun it was because you did not look at it?'

"Yeah, I knew it was a 12-bore"

"And how did you know it was a 12-bore?"

"'Cos Ray told me it was and I could feel it through the sacking."

"Have you ever held a 12-bore before or used one?"

"No, course not."

"Yet you're willing to tell this court that you knew it was a 12-bore, simply on your friend Ray's word and on your feel of it?"

"Yeah."

"And is your friend Ray a gun expert?"

"You'd have to ask him that"

"Really. Ray's a heroin addict too, isn't he?"

There was a visible stir on the faces of some of the jury.

"You'd have to ask him that."

Crehan paused. He was warming to the task and seemed to know exactly where to point his questions.

"This supposed day when in broad daylight you brought a lethal weapon to me wrapped only in sacking through the streets of Stetchworth, what were you wearing?"

"I can't remember."

"What do you mean, you can't remember, do you carry guns and ammunition around town every day?"

"No, I just can't remember what I was wearing. It was probably jeans and a jumper."

"What colour jumper?"

"Probably blue but I can't remember, like I said."

"And describe my car to me"

"It's not a car, it's a Transit"

"Colour?"

"I can't remember. White maybe"

"And how did you pass this gun and ammunition to me?"

"I got in your passenger seat and you told me to leave it on the floor."

"And who put you up to all this?'

"Nobody put me up to this, you know it's what happened."

Crehan paused.

"Now let's turn to your episode in the cells at Stetchworth Police station. From what we have heard you are asking this court to seriously believe that you were taken by the police and transported into the cells below the station without being told why you were there, or cautioned or anything? That's totally ridiculous!"

"It sounds crazy but that's the truth of what I remember."

"Isn't the real truth, which I put to you, that you had informed on me for some reason and the police had put you in the cells in order to get me to make some kind of admission. To verbal me up. Isn't that the truth of what really happened?"

The judge coughed and looked up.

"Mr Crehan, I'm not sure this is taking you very far. I have allowed you to make your point and you have made it to the witness most forcefully. As you know, you will have another opportunity to return to what happened in the police cells. I suggest it is in your interests to keep your powder dry until that moment comes."

Chambers was nodding at Crehan and he visibly relented.

"Very well, Your Honour."

At this point the judge raised his head.

"Mr Crehan, I am presuming that you are now approaching the end of your questions. Your advisers will speak to you as to what you should now be formally putting to this witness."

Chambers was already whispering to Crehan who looked up at the witness

"This is a pack of lies, Mr Graham, isn't it? I put it to you that you were never asked to obtain a gun of any kind by me, that you never delivered a gun and ammunition to me and that you certainly never met me in Bedwell Crescent or entered my van to deliver any gun and ammunition"

"You know I did"

"Any re-examination?" directed the judge to Ableman.

"Just two questions, Your Honour,"

"Go ahead"

"Mr Graham, it is understandable that our recollections of past events get fuzzy over time and I don't wish to suggest that given your own particular circumstances your memory is worst than most but first, are you sure about the colour of your jumper that day, and second, the colour of the van that you say Mr Crehan was driving?"

"Yeah, I'm pretty sure it must have been a blue jumper 'cos I only have a couple and my favourite is blue. And yeah, his van is a white Transit".

"And is it possible your memory may be playing tricks on you?"

"Nah, I don't think so"

"Very well, we'll leave it there"

Ableman sat down, inwardly seething and conscious of the entire defence team smiling at him.

The mood in the post session debrief in Crehan's holding cell that evening was much improved.

"I have to say, Pat, that for a rank amateur you are taking to cross examination like a duck to water," said Chambers, slapping the defendant on the back. "It was almost as though you knew you were leading Ableman into that disastrous re-exam. Well done."

"Yeah , I couldn't believe he got Graham to repeat the errors to the jury twice. He must know it will sow doubts after Paddy O'Neill gives his evidence. Makes me wonder what they will try and dig up to distract from it."

"Well we'll see. It will be Ray Johnson first thing in the morning. He's only material against us if the jury accept he is part of the chain supplying the murder weapon for you so tread carefully as you attack him. We discussed this at length with Semken so you know the issues."

There was a rap at the door which signalled it was time for Crehan to board the prison van taking him back to Brixton. A quick exchange of farewells and a chorus of "well-dones" followed him out of the door.

Chambers gestured for Feargal and Steve to stay.

"Lads, a few things. Well done today. It went better than we could have hoped for and in no little part due to your hard work. But I sense Pat is very close to the threshold of losing his cool. He did well today and we got lucky with some inept questioning but I am sure Oliver will be tightening everything up from now on. Feargal have you got that certified copy of the Transit's registration?"

"Yes, Boss"

"And it clearly says blue as the colour?"

"It does."

"And we have the evidence from the guy in Preston that it was still blue when he bought it from Pat in October?"

"Yes."

"OK. That's all for now. We shall see how the next few days go. Feargal, one more thing and consider this a bollocking.

We do not show any facial or bodily expression whatsoever when evidence goes for or against us. We have no idea of the effect that has on the jury so we keep it locked down. Do you understand?"

"Yes, Boss. Sorry."

"No worries, it's your first big trial. We all have to learn. Steve, I'll see you here in the morning at nine. Feargal, please go to the office and bring any mail over that Mrs Peach feels I should see. We need you here for 9.30."

With that the team separated and headed back to their normal lives which it seemed had been placed in suspended animation for a week or two. Outside the summer was passing quickly. The short test series against New Zealand had resulted in victory for the home side and Illingworth and his men were being touted as capable of dealing with the West Indies side about to arrive with such luminaries as Lloyd, Sobers and Kallicharan amongst them. But for Feargal, normally a cricket obsessive, his new role as an important member of the Crehan defence team made everything else pale into insignificance.

Ray Johnson had enjoyed a harsh life to date. Found abandoned in the East End of London he had spent a childhood in and out of foster homes and council funded care homes for children. He had come to Stetchworth at the age of 8 and attended a local junior school where he was deemed to be of average intelligence and had then been sent to the local secondary modern school where he found it hard to make friends and even harder to study. By the age of 14 he had graduated from some petty vandalism and shoplifting to taking and driving away cars. The need to inject excitement into an uncared for and unloved life soon led him to experiment with drugs and by his late teens Ray had served two short terms at Young Offender institutions and worse had developed a severe heroin habit. Essentially a loner, Ray had found companionship with other small-time criminals in Stetchworth and the surrounding towns and had acted as lookout on various burglaries and had graduated in time to providing the transport for some of the criminal enterprises in the area. He was short of friends however and their joint loneliness and dependence on drugs had drawn John Graham and him together. They met regularly when attending the methadone clinic

Ray was an unimposing figure in the witness box. Five foot seven and of slight build he already had thin light brown hair pulled back, teddy-boy style and his eyes were shielded by tinted clear-framed yellow spectacles through which he squinted at Ableman who tortuously dragged out the evidence from him.

The story according to Ray was that his good friend Graham had asked him if he knew where he could acquire a firearm for some criminal business. He had assumed it was to be used in an armed robbery somewhere and would need to be totally untraceable. He had heard about a dealer in Ware who sold hunting rifles and shotguns for a living but was also rumoured to ply a secret trade in weapons for the underworld on a strictly cash basis. It had not been simple but Ray had managed to obtain a 12-bore with cartridges which he had supplied to Graham. He had paid the supplier and pocketed twenty quid for his trouble and had then delivered the gun to Graham's house wrapped in a sack. No, he was not a police informant and had no fears that Graham was one either. Yes he knew the victim and the defendant

When Johnson was finally his for cross examination, and Ableman had taken his seat, Crehan was gentle. There was no point in trying to prove that Johnson was lying. Better to let the jury have a first row view of the quality of the evidence upon which they were relying. Johnson was less haughty about his drugs usage and openly admitted to be a heroin user that was now trying to get his life back under control by partaking willingly of the methadone programme. Yes he had numerous convictions for dishonesty. They were all in the past. Yes, he was aware that he had committed a serious crime in supplying a firearm that was unregistered to a known criminal. Yes he knew Graham had no shotgun licence. The police had assured him that if he gave evidence along the lines of his statement, he would not be prosecuted for the crime.

"So you've come along here today to give evidence in order to save your own skin, would that be true Mr Johnson?"

"Yes, but what I have told the court is true."

"Of course it is." Crehan ended and sat down.

"That is probably a convenient time for a short break. Members of the jury, 15 minutes." Thus said the judge and hurried out of the court. The courtroom relaxed as the jury exited for tea or coffee and the defence team gathered around the dock.

The period between the resumption after the coffee break and the adjournment for lunch was taken up with the acceptance into evidence of the statement of the Scenes of Crime Officer and the officer who had visited the location where the alleged murder weapon had been found by a group of young boys playing in undergrowth.

The Statement of the Scenes of Crime Officer was unremarkable. It brought into evidence everything that had been taken from the road floor in the vicinity of the shooting soon after the murder had occurred and included the tabs from within the spent cartridges, various chewing gum wrappers of the "Wrigley's Spearmint" variety, a number of nails and rags, a tyre valve cap, and various other pieces of inconsequential litter.

The evidence of the officer at the location of the gun discovery was more interesting. He acknowledged that the young boys had recognized that they had found a real gun and had been too frightened to touch it "in case it went off." He had accompanied them back to the scene where he had discovered a 12-bore shotgun in its three constituent parts neatly stowed under a hedge in fairly thick undergrowth at the edge of a green where local boys often played games.

During the lunch break Crehan and Chambers discussed this.

"I can't believe they are going to try and make something out of the wrappers. Talk about clutching at straws…"

"I know Pat, but it may well work in our favour. The jury seem interested and don't want to be led by the nose. Let's be patient and see what Austin says when she gives evidence."

"Yeah, I'm more interested in the gun location. It's on a direct line between the shooting and my home. It's almost as if they looked at the map and decided where I would have dumped the weapon. It's a real stinking fit-up. I really think we should insist on looking at the location. Can you get that young lad of yours to go up there and scout around?"

"Let's make it official and ask the judge to direct the officer… McQueen… to show Feargal exactly where it was found…?"

Judge Antrim-Davies was surprisingly receptive that the Scenes of Crime Officer assigned to the case should demonstrate to a representative of both prosecution and defence the exact location where the shotgun had been discovered. In the circumstances Ableman who had initially seemed irritated by the suggestion was forced albeit grudgingly to agree and an appointment was set for the following Monday at 10.

During the remainder of the afternoon a police sergeant, Lily Austin, gave evidence that she had been requested to clean the cell occupied by Pat Crehan once he had been taken from Stetchworth Police Station to the local Magistrates Court to be first publicly accused of the crime for which he now stood trial. Austin produced the contents in a large polythene bag with an Exhibit number and inventory. The puzzlement of the introduction of this evidence was clear on the faces of both the judge and the jury but was not lost on the defence. The judge peered quizzically at Ableman.

"Your Honour, you will see that Items 9 to 17 in the inventory are the inner and outer wrappers of separate sticks of Spearmint Gum made by Wrigley's and consumed by the defendant whilst he was the sole occupant of Holding Cell 5 at Stetchworth Police Station. The relevance of this evidence, Your Honour, is that you will recall that a similar wrapper was recovered from the immediate vicinity of the murder scene."

"Is there anything you wish to say concerning the introduction of this exhibit, Mr Crehan?" The judge looked at Crehan who was shaking his head.

"They're having a laugh, Your Honour. This is absolutely ridiculous."

"Mr Ableman," the judge addressed the experienced Queen's Counsel, "I fully appreciate that the Crown's case is built entirely on evidence which is circumstantial, but I fail to see how any reasonable jury would attach any credence to this evidence whatsoever. You've introduced it now and it will stay but I can tell you that I shall direct the jury to properly disregard it when the time comes for their deliberation."

"Very well, Your Honour." Ableman sat down and quickly turned behind to those instructing him. It was a scowl that said, "I told you so."

The day ended there. Bridget was able to steal five minutes with Pat in the cells below and take his court suit home for cleaning with two dirty shirts. Chambers then saw his client for a further few minutes. They had achieved what they had wanted with the first week's evidence and more perhaps but there was still a huge mountain to climb. Nonetheless all went their respective ways exhausted but satisfied that they had done everything they could.

Feargal was home at his parents by six and was playing football with the group of local lads who always congregated on the green at the bottom of the road where he lived on a Friday night by 6.30. The game was fun and by 7.30 the ten or so boys were as was usual laying on the raised grass at the back of the green which in turn overlooked the playing fields of one of the local schools. Little did they know that in ten years' time the playing fields and the meadows beyond them would all have been eaten up by the relentless expansion of Stetchworth. Tonight, all talk was of the Crehan murder trial. Feargal couldn't believe it. These lads with whom he had grown up and who were all in the first couple of years of their apprenticeships or were in their final years at school were not exactly on top of current affairs. They rarely read a newspaper and certainly never watched the news on television, yet each one of them without exception had read every page of the reporting in the local newspapers and knew the names of all the protagonists to date. All of them knew Feargal's involvement but he had told them from the start that he could not discuss the case with them and he had been true to his word so far. Opinion was divided amongst the group as to whether Pat was guilty or not. There was definitely a current that said there were too many coincidences that pointed towards his guilt… no smoke without fire… but these were after all just ordinary guys who had never brushed up against the law and did not hold perhaps as much cynicism about the police as men who had. One of the boys, Mark, was the same age as Feargal and had just started as a clerk at the same law firm, in fact Feargal had been instrumental in getting him through to a second interview with Chambers himself.

"What's the feeling at the office?" Feargal asked Mark when they were walking together back to their homes.

"Oh, it's pretty mixed really mate. Usual gossip. Of course a lot just assume he is guilty and more think he must be if Geoffrey is defending him. You know the score!"

"I've been trying to get you involved in it all. There might be an opportunity next week. Be ready!"

Feargal left Mark to go into his house and walked up the rest of the road to where his house was. As he neared the front of the house, he noticed that his father's car came round the corner, swung into the short drive in front of the house and his father jumped out.

"Ferg, you're back already! Are you coming in the house?"

They both pushed through the gate which led to the alley past the garage and brought them to the back of the house and the kitchen. In the kitchen, his mother was cooking.

"Hi mum." He leaned and kissed her

"Hi darling, I presume you are in for dinner. How has today gone?"

"Give him a chance, woman," his father admonished her, "let him get in and washed first, we'll get all the news later."

His mother raised her eyebrows and shook her head and Feargal smiled.

"Dinner in ten minutes."

Dinner was a fairly basic meal. Mum's standard shepherd's pie and peas, but was hot and filling and was followed by a homemade treacle tart and custard. Feargal's sister Onya was away in London so there were only the three of them. His parents, like the boys on the green, had read everything connected with the trial and had witnessed a short piece on the television which had outlined some of the early evidence. They were the kind of parents every child wanted. They were totally supportive, sometimes beyond objectivity, but Feargal knew that it was from that love and support that he gained his confidence. He knew he would have their backing whatever he chose to do in life. He also knew that, since he was working for Geoffrey Chambers, whom his parents wholeheartedly believed in, they would already have assumed that Crehan was innocent and all the evidence against him was a concoction.

Such was the tone of the conversation between the three of them that in the interests of common sense, Feargal found himself taking the side of the prosecution. Why would Graham and Johnson lie about the gun? What axe did Mrs Appletree have to grind? How did the residue get on the coat? Mum and Dad were convinced already however and it came almost as a relief when his mother remembered that his friend Clive had dropped in for a cup of tea that afternoon and asked her to remind him that his friends were all meeting in the bar at The Cromwell at 8.30.

"You'll need to get a move on then. Don't be too late. None of these three o'clock jobs. You'll be tired and need a good night's sleep. And be careful, the whole town is talking about this case and some will know that you are involved in it. Remember there's nowt so strange as folk."

"I know, Dad, I'll be careful. And I am tired."

Human beings were strange, he reflected, as he drove his beaten-up old Ford 100E down to Stetchworth Old Town, the collection of old Tudor buildings which flanked the old Roman Road that eventually became the A1 the essential artery to the North from London. Stetchworth New Town had been tacked on and around the famous Old Town, much to the chagrin of its long-time residents and there was definitely a feel of 'them and us' towards the thousands of young families now settling in the newly built areas. Feargal knew the Old Town well. There had been a grammar school there since 1558 and he had been privileged to attend. It was fully three miles from home and the journey to and from interesting whether by bike bus car or on foot and often complicated by the need to travel in uniform which set you out to the bully boys and also the boys from the Roman Catholic grammar school, St Michaels, which was in Hitchin. That meant the Stetchworth boys attending St Micks, as it was known, were forced to travel on the 303 bus which stopped in the Old Town. Boys at Feargal's school had been well advised to travel in groups. Woe betide a careless and tired boy thoughtlessly wandering on to the top deck of the 303 to find a dozen or so of the Hitchin contingent lying in wait for him. Such folly always resulted in a weekend trip to the Outfitters in the Town Centre to acquire, at least, a new cap with the red Tudor rose badge for mother to sew on, and probably a new blazer to boot. Yes, how strange that the entire town of some 25,000 plus were obsessed with the guilt or innocence of Pat Crehan, but incredibly few had been thinking of the dreadful trauma suffered by Jo Blake, the loss for her family and their future struggles. Still fewer had even mentioned Bridget and the family and what they must be going through. Stetchworth was like a big overgrown dysfunctional family. Relatives were everywhere and rumours spread like wildfire. Feargal mused that it was because everyone in the New Town was trying to build a new life and had come together from all parts that that common experience had helped knit a camaraderie that was constantly apparent. Why, he thought, was it that in this close-knit community there had been no mention of any kind of motive that Pat Crehan may have had to callously lie in wait for Tony Blake and coolly blast him to death?

Feargal parked in the car park of The Cromwell, an old coaching inn converted into a hotel, whose large long low-raftered bar was now the meeting place of choice for Stetchworth youngsters of a certain age. There were already a lot of people in the bar and as he pushed open the door he heard several conversations immediately go quiet and then resume again as he walked past. He realized that people knew he was involved and everyone was talking about it.

He saw some of his friends at the end of the bar. Steve was there with the brothers Jim and Gerry and by the time he reached them, Dick and Clive had followed him into the bar, He had joined this bunch of friends since leaving school. He had known all of them for many years but Steve, who was a conveyancing clerk at the law firm, was the catalyst who had brought them all together with Feargal and he was enjoying knowing them. None were from similar backgrounds but all bar Feargal were out working for a living. All enjoyed the same sense of humour.

"Rita," greeted Steve. He had decided that Feargal resembled the actress Rita Tushingham and the description had stuck,

"What do you want Ferg?" Jim was always the first to the bar and always direct.

"Light and bitter please Jim."

Dick and Clive caught up with them.

"Ah, tis the Talk of the Town," he looked at Feargal.

"Yeah yeah yeah. We'll soon be yesterday's news."

"I wouldn't be so sure of that, mate. Nobody's talking about anything else at the moment. And how much longer is it going to last?"

"I think it will be over next week"

"So did he do it Ferg?" Jim was as direct as ever.

"I don't think they have any evidence to allow a jury to convict."

"Yeah but that's not the question. Do you think he did it?"

"I have no idea."

"Spoken like a true lawyer. You should go and do a law degree."

"Very funny."

They all knew he was about to go up to Oxford in October to study law. In fact they had all celebrated with him when he got the letter telling him that he had gained admission. Although he had not known them long, he knew they were on his side and took great pleasure from his success. He was sure they would be up at Oxford regularly and that all would be friends for a very long time.

The banter continued way into the night and when he finally hit the pillow in the early hours Feargal's last thought before the exhaustion took over was how he could never have contemplated being a bit player in this major event that was clearly taking over Stetchworth.

The Saturday saw him turning out for Stetchworth 2nd XI playing on the main Stetchworth pitch on the London Road. He bowled a few overs and scored some runs but his mind wasn't fully on the cricket and it showed.

Sunday passed uneventfully. He accompanied his father to the school at which he was the headmaster. A few of the teachers were there with whom he still enjoyed a great rapport and he was pleased to see them but everyone simply wanted to know what was going to happen next, and he was unable to tell them.

And so Monday arrived and he found himself at the location of the shotgun discovery. He was first there although there were already some kids paying an impromptu game of football on the grass. Eventually Sergeant McQueen showed up. He and Feargal actually knew each other through a mutual friend of his father. One of the lawyers from the Crown service arrived and they walked over as directed by the officer who carried a piece of wood wrapped in a sack to imitate the gun and placed it in position. A sketch map was going to be made available and Feargal took some Polaroid pictures of the position with the camera loaned to him by the firm.

As soon as he saw where McQueen had placed the gun he knew there was trouble ahead, as probably did the solicitor from the Crown Service.

He thanked the officer and made his excuses and left to hot-tail it over to St Albans to the courthouse where he knew the proverbial was going to collide with the fan. But he couldn't deliver his message straightaway for there was plenty of action already going on in Court.

In the witness box was the large , rotund, balding figure of Detective Sergeant Bob Jones and he was about to be passed over for cross examination by Crehan. According to his original deposition, and it was unlikely that Ableman would have taken him far from that in his evidence in chief, Jones and Detective Constable Barry Barlow had both secreted themselves in a cell at Stetchworth Police Station on the night of November 6th. It was the penultimate cell in the row of five cells below the working floor of the station. They knew that Crehan was in the cell at the far end, although they had waited for him to be taken out briefly for an interview, and they were also were aware that John Graham was about to be brought in and would be placed in the cell at the end next to them. Jones' evidence was that there was then a conversation between the two men of an incriminating nature that he and Barlow compiled details of immediately afterwards in their notebooks.

The conversation went as follows according to the officer:

NOISE

"Who's that?" PC

"Who's that?" JG

"Is that you John?" PC

"Yeah. Pat?" JG

"Yeah, What the fuck are you doing down here?" PC

"They're saying it was you done for Tony and have me as an accomplice." JG

"That's total bollocks. It was nothing to do with me." PC

"They're asking me about the shooter." JG

"Just keep your mouth shut." PC

"They know all about it, Pat. For definate." JG

"Keep your fucking mouth shut or you'll regret it. I promise." PC

PAUSE

"Have you got a brief?" PC

"Nah, course not." JG

"Fucking get one and don't say a word without him being there." PC

That was the entirety of the supposed conversation and, on the face of it, it wasn't too compromising for Pat's defence case. Feargal had no doubt that Saltpetre would have taken a very soft approach with the officer but Crehan was not going to let it go.

"So Detective Sergeant Jones, I would like you to take a look at the deposition of Detective Constable Barlow which appears at page 321 of the Court Bundle."

Jones was handed the copy and studied it.

"Yes?"

"What do you notice about it?"

"His account of what was said is the same as mine."

"Yes, it's exactly the same as yours, word for word."

"Well, it would be, wouldn't it as we both heard the same conversation?"

"You typed this up from your notebook notes how much later?"

"I would guess it was about ten minutes after we left the cells that we made up our notes and I typed mine up when I came back on shift the following day."

"And your colleague?"

"Well, I can't speak for him but I suggest he did more or less the same."

"So you did not make up your notes together?"

"No."

"You're certain of that?"

"Absolutely."

"Would you please have a look at your notebook. I want you to go to the place where you spell the word 'definite'."

"Yes, I have found it."

"You have spelt it wrong."

"Oh yes."

"And you definitely compiled your notes of what you heard together with your colleague DC Barlow?'

"No. Certainly not."

"How do you explain then, that you have both spelt 'definite' incorrectly in exactly the same way?"

"I can't explain it."

"Had you noticed it before today?"

"No."

"No, I thought not. You two simply prepared this version of what was said in the cells together, didn't you?"

"No we did not."

"And it's a coincidence as well is it that John Graham's version, he being a witness on whose truthfulness the Crown depends, is completely different to yours?"

"Well, I don't suppose he was making notes at the time."

"Neither were you by your own admission. I have no further questions for this lying toad, Your Honour."

"Mr Crehan. I will not have witnesses abused in my courtroom. Let's have no further outbursts like that. You will have every opportunity of addressing the jury in due course. Now, Mr Ableman, any re-examination?"

"None, your Honour. I call the next witness, Detective Constable Barry Barlow."

Barlow came in to Court, took the oath and Ableman took him through his evidence. Once he had concluded Pat took a different path with him.

"So you had secreted yourself in the cell with Detective Sergeant Jones before anyone else was placed in the cells?'

"That's correct"

"So how did you know that it was John Graham and myself speaking?"

"Of course I knew, because we had agreed a plan with the custody officers that they would bring you and Graham down and place you in those cells."

"You'd agreed a plan? And what was the plan?"

"To listen to whatever conversation took place."

"In the hope that one or the other of us would confess to Tony Blake's murder?"

"In the hope it would further our investigations."

"And why didn't you record it? It's common knowledge that you record most conversations at Stetchworth Nick?'

"That's not true but we could not record it because the tape recorder is too noisy and may have alerted you to the fact that we were there."

"How very convenient. So the only version we have is what you and Detective Sergeant Jones compiled together later when you made up your notes?"

"That's not true either. We made our notebooks up separately."

"Oh really? And when and where did you make up your notes?"

"It would have been about an hour later and in my office."

"Can you be definite about that?

"Yes, very definite.'

"Just one last thing. Please indulge the court and spell the word definite."

Barlow looked at the prosecution team quizzically and then at the judge for some guidance but none was forthcoming.

"Come on, or you'll never pass your Sergeant's exams!"

The judge scowled at Crehan.

"Well, my spelling is not my strong point but I think it is D.E.F.I.N.I.T.E."

"That's right. And the reason you have spelt it wrong in your notes is because you were copying DS Jones' notes weren't you?"

"No, that's not true."

"I have no further questions Your Honour."

Ableman rose wearily to his feet.

"Detective Constable Barlow. To the best of your knowledge, were there any individuals in custody at Stetchworth Police Station on this evening in question?"

"No, sir"

"And when you made up your notes to record what took place in the cells, the events were still fresh in your mind?"

"Yes, sir."

"And could it just be possible that you spelt the word 'definite' incorrectly by complete accident and because as you said, spelling is not your strong point?"

"I'm sure that's the case, sir."

"Thank you. Unless Your Honour has any further questions…?"

Antrim-Davies shook his head and Barlow left the witness box and then the Court

The judge ordered the lunch break, requiring everyone to be back in their seats by 2.30 and the defence team gathered around the dock.

Chambers was pleased with the way the evidence of the two policemen had gone. 'Verbals' as the common practice of police officers to put words in the mouths of suspected offenders by accusing them of saying things that incriminated them had been around forever and was despicable. However it showed that the real evidence from neutral parties was not strong. He was pleased at the sensible way Crehan had cross examined them and felt he had detected some irritation on the faces of one or two jury members. Steve confirmed that he had seen one member, the burly man with the moustache at position 11, visibly shake his head on a couple of the denials from the witness box.

They turned to Feargal who had yet to report on the position of the gun when it was discovered. He showed the photographs of the bushes surrounding the spot and the rough map that had been supplied that morning.

"The long and short of it is that the shotgun has not been casually hidden or been tossed into the hedgerow as they would like us to accept. The surrounding trees and bushes are a mixture of hawthorn and beech. It's very green now but I think that even in early November anyone placing the gun where it was found would have probably torn their coat or at least been covered with bits of old foliage etcetera"

"How do we get this in as evidence?" asked Pat

"Let's have a think about it, but worst case you could call Ferg as a witness?"

They parked the thought and quickly moved on to the next concern which was the upcoming evidence of Paddy O'Neill. Paddy was an ex-traffic policeman who had been retired early from the force on ill-health grounds when he had suffered a catastrophic head injury whilst on duty. He and his co-driver on Motorway Patrol had attended a breakdown on the A1 Motorway between Stetchworth and Letchworth. A van had broken down and had managed to manoeuvre on to the hard shoulder. Paddy had the bonnet open and was trying to find the cause of the breakdown when a lorry driver fell asleep at the wheel lower down the road and ploughed into the back of the patrol car which in turn cannoned into the back of the van. Paddy was extremely lucky to be alive and underwent extensive cranial surgery. He had been discharged from the force but rumour was that the police union was up in arms on his behalf at the paucity of compensation he had been offered.

He spoke slowly but there was no suggestion that his brain wasn't working properly. Essentially the evidence that O'Neill was tortuously led through by Ableman was that he had been walking one Saturday morning from his home in Shephall

View to pick up the newspaper and some bread from the Bedwell shops. According to O'Neill, when he was about 50 yards from a blue ford Transit, he saw the passenger door open, and a known criminal and police informant, John Graham, dropped out of the door and walked away at which the van drove off. For some reason O'Neill was suspicious and decided to remember the Registration Number of the Transit which was FEG 373. He then contacted a friend at the police station who had advised him that the van was registered in the name of Patrick Crehan, a name also familiar to O'Neill.

When it was announced that Crehan had been arrested in connection with the murder of Tony Blake, O'Neill had decided to report what he had seen to the investigating team.

And so Pat Crehan commenced his cross examination of what seemed a fairly damning witness confirming the link between John Graham and Pat Crehan and demonstrating the truth behind at least part of Graham's evidence.

"Mr O'Neill. Let me ask you. Do you make a habit of logging times when you see someone familiar on the street?"

"No, but when I see criminals that I know, I do tend to make a mental note of when I saw them."

"Even when they are harmlessly getting in and out of cars?"

"Yes."

"So, please give the court a flavour of just how often that is. For example, how often have you made a mental note of seeing someone you consider suspicious on your everyday dog walk, between say, then and now?"

"Well I don't think I have since then, Stetchworth is a fairly peaceful place normally and nothing much happens."

"So in the last six months the only time you have mentally recorded an event was when you say you saw John Graham getting out of a Ford Transit in Bedwell and all he was doing was getting out of a passenger door and walking away?"

"Yes, that's correct.'

"And you were about 50 yards away?"

"I guess I was about 50 yards behind the van at this stage."

"And how did you recognize Mr Graham?"

"I recognized him from his long hair and knew it was him straight away."

"Seriously?'

"Yes"

"And did you recognize the driver?"

"No."

"You said in your deposition that he was wearing a red pullover, yet today you were far less sure, why is that?"

"I think it was red but the counsel earlier sowed some doubts in my mind."

"So now you are not so sure? But you are sure that it was John Graham?"

"Yes I am certain."

"You have recently been released from the police force, have you not?"

"Yes, as I explained in my evidence earlier.'

"And that was because you received serious and traumatic injuries to your neck and head from which you are not yet fully recovered?"

"Well I consider that I am fully recovered but the doctors advise that I am unfit ever to resume full duties."

"And when did this dreadful accident take place?"

"A year and ten days ago."

"So you were not long out of hospital on the day you say you saw Graham?"

"I'd been out for a month or so."

"Three weeks and two days in fact... I have the details of your discharge home here... and you were in almost daily outpatient care...?'

"Yes, that's true."

"Yet you still felt the devotion to duty to note down the totally innocent activity of getting out of a car by a known criminal at a time when surely your focus must have been that you were lucky to be alive?"

"Yes I did, and I am here today as a result."

"Isn't the truth of this matter that in order to make this whole pack of lies believable, someone, probably an old colleague, realized that they had better get me and Graham spotted together and you are the patsy they chose to do it?"

"No, that's just not so."

"What did they threaten you with? No pension? Some old misdemeanour?"

"Nobody threatened me."

Antrim-Davies was clearly coming to an end of his patience with the line of questioning, but Crehan continued.

"You see, Mr O'Neill, the point is I personally know you are lying. I know I was never in Bedwell on that day and I certainly know that you never saw John Graham alight from my Transit. I know you are lying and fairly soon the jury too will know that you are lying. Before I explain to you why I know you are lying please explain to the jury again how you were able to remember my number plate when you finally returned home? You have already told the court that you did not write it down at the time."

O'Neill again explained that his memory had been impaired by his accident and that he had used a set of mnemonics to remember the letters and some number associations to remember the three digits.

"Mr O'Neill, I personally fitted a towbar to the Transit in August last year. I didn't do a very good job because the towbar plate obscures most of the registration plate which I never got round to moving. It is impossible to read the number plate accurately from even ten yards away. I have been stopped twice by Stetchworth traffic police about this. What do you say to that?"

"I could see the plate clearly."

"Bullshit," Pat ended

Ableman re-examined and had O'Neill repeat how sure he was that he had seen the plate clearly and had no cause to give any kind of malicious or false evidence against Crehan.

It was 3.50 pm and the judge looked at Ableman.

"Mr Ableman, I sense we are coming to the end of the case

for the prosecution. Should we continue or would now be a convenient time to adjourn?"

"Your Honour, there are a few more matters. There are a number of exhibits to enter into evidence, none of which are contentious. The defence have asked that I tender the officer leading this investigation, Detective Superintendent Kenneth Oliver, to answer one or possibly two relevant questions. He is present and willing to so do and so I suggest we deal with that after which the exhibits can be admitted and we can adjourn. Tomorrow I will call the widow of the victim and her evidence will conclude the prosecution case."

"Very well," the Judge agreed.

Ken Oliver took the stand and was sworn in. He was relieved that he was not about to be cross examined by some smart-arse QC but it had been reported back to him that Crehan, aided by Chambers was doing a competent job of defending himself.

Ableman began, "DCS Oliver, I do not have any questions for you although I may need to re-examine you should anything arise from the question you are about to be asked. Please wait there."

"Mine is a simple question DCS Oliver. On the 6th November 1972, I was arrested at my home by officers acting at your direction and eventually charged with the murder of Tony Blake, of which I am innocent. It is clear from all witness statements that, at the time of my arrest, you possessed no evidence, even of a totally circumstantial nature, to suggest to you that I might have been the perpetrator of the offence, so please explain to this courtroom why and for what reason I was so roughly handled and arrested?"

Oliver may have been ruffled but he certainly did not show it. His rise through the ranks had been assured and his poise did not desert him now.

"A warrant was issued for your arrest on suspicion of being involved in the murder of Tony Blake after we received information from a reliable source that you were so involved."

"And who was that source?"

"It was a reliable informant."

"And what was his or her name?"

"I cannot reveal the name of the informant."

"So I have been subjected to this torture, and now face a possible life term because of some grass who you refuse to name?"

Oliver looked to the Judge who predictably rode swiftly to his rescue.

"Ladies and gentlemen of the jury, the police often solve major crimes as a result of information given to them either anonymously or by members of the criminal fraternity. It would be disastrous for them if they were forced to name the informant on each occasion. That is not to say that they do not have to then proceed to prove their case. However, there is nothing unusual in the position stated by Detective Chief Superintendent Oliver.'

"That is disgusting. No further questions."

Feargal may have wondered what the point of that exchange was, but noted that Chambers was very approving of the line that Crehan had taken. The jury were on their way home for another evening. There was only Jo Blake to take the stand in the morning after which the prosecution would close its case. Pat then would have to open the defence case There was a discussion of a submission at the halfway point of "No Case to Answer." Chambers expected Crehan to want to make the submission which effectively said, "They've failed even to raise the faintest of cases against me," but that was not so.

"I want to get Feargal's evidence in and you are going to have to fetch the Transit down."

"Sure. You need to consider whether you are going to give evidence…"

"Yep, I'll make a decision in the morning. What do you think?"

"Honestly, I think we might be winning this and I don't want to fuck it up with Ableman going into your previous and so on. I know you're smart but I don't think it's a risk worth taking."

"What's my evidence going to be?" asked Feargal

"I just want you to say in your own words where the gun was found. Nothing more."

"And don't get clever with Ableman," said Steve

"Then I want you to get up to Preston and fetch the Transit back. The office has already cleared it with the new owner. Take Mark with you. Take the office Opel."

"Can't I take your Vitesse?"

"Fuck off."

They all chuckled. The case was about to get very difficult but at least they were now in the driving seat.

Tuesday began with Jo Blake in the stand. She had been at the court all week along with other members of her family. The defence team members could feel the hatred every time they walked past them outside the court or in the coffee shop below. It was a mystery to Feargal, but he presumed they had been fed a story by the police who were adamant that they had the right man.

It seemed the prosecution had introduced her evidence not for its weight against Pat but for the prejudicial effect of the horror of the night of the murder. Jo had not seen anything material but she had experienced the whole nightmare. She was asked if she knew Pat and confirmed that she did and that to her certain knowledge Tony had passed work Pat's way. She was keen to let the court know however that her Tony regarded Pat as a liar and untrustworthy and that there was some recent bad blood between the two of them. Pat was probably mistaken to try and cross examine her. She was hostile from the start. When asked eventually why she was so upset she took her chance.

"When they first arrested you, I was sure that you would not have killed my Tony. In fact I did not believe you had the balls for it, but now I have listened to all the evidence I have no doubts at all that you pulled the trigger that night. I hope you rot in hell."

It was Feargal's turn immediately after the morning coffee break. He felt his legs trembling as he declared that he wished to affirm and as he lifted his right arm along the raised side of the witness box, he felt rivulets of sweat form and drip into the armpit of his shirt.

Pat got him through the evidence that he wanted the court to hear. The gun had been secreted in thick undergrowth, not casually thrown in there. It would have been impossible for a large man of any size over five feet to place the gun where it had been found without having to fight through bushes and thorns. He had waited to be cross examined, not really expecting his evidence to be doubted, but Ableman was in no mood to let this pass through.

Feargal couldn't really understand why Ableman wanted to call his honesty and accuracy of recollection into question and yet for 20 minutes the experienced QC kept returning to his evidence in chief and tried to turn it around or confuse the location of the gun. Feargal felt he was equal to it and yet was grateful when, with one final theatrical sigh and roll of the eyebrows, the Silk gave up the struggle.

Feargal returned to the seats alongside Geoff and was gratified to see Steve nodding and hear a whispered "Well done" from Geoff.

If he had been in the courtroom at the start of the afternoon session, Feargal would have heard the judge advise the court that the jury, presumably as a result of his evidence, wished to visit and inspect the location where the gun was found. A coach would need to be arranged and the inspection was scheduled for the Wednesday afternoon at 2 pm. Feargal heard none of this. He had already gone back to Stetchworth and changed for the drive with Mark to Preston in Lancashire for a prearranged meeting with the owner of the famous blue Ford Transit van.

Julian, who owned the Transit turned out to be a pleasure to meet. He was originally from the Stetchworth area and had been following the murder and subsequent trial in the press and via his in-laws who still lived in the area. He had met Pat when he had collected the Transit in late October and had found him uncomplicated to deal with. He was amazed at how events had unfolded. He insisted on buying them some fish and chips for the journey back and presumed he would see them again when they returned to collect the Opel Kadett later in the week. It had taken the two boys about three and a half hours to drive up from Stetchworth and they felt that four hours was a realistic journey time back which would get them back to Stetchworth at about midnight.

"You shouldn't have any trouble with her. I've filled her up with petrol. I have had no problems with her at all since I bought her. Safe journey, Lads and good luck with the trial." He patted the side of the window and Feargal started the drive back. He was used to driving Ford Transits. He had in fact learned to drive in the school's bus which was used to travel all of the school sports teams to away fixtures when required. At weekends he would often drive around the school grounds whilst his father fed the animals or did something or other and would practise his reversing and parking. The net result was that he was able to pass his driving test first time and very soon after his 17th birthday and was now used to driving a few different kinds of vehicles.

Mark was not so experienced. He had passed his test though and Feargal had promised him he could drive at some stage on the journey as a bribe to ensure his company.

As it was the journey was easy. The boys stopped at a Services on the M6 just past Wolverhampton and Mark drove the rest of the way home. The Transit was sound except for a less than precise steering wheel. The journey was however full of tense anticipation caused certainly by the knowledge obtained almost immediately upon arrival that the towbar did exactly what Crehan had said it did.

"It's in a really bad position," remarked Julian

You would need x-ray eyes to discern the actual number of the van from anything more than two or three yards behind it.

Feargal had already telephoned Geoff from Julian's house phone to let him know as much. He had tried to contain his excitement and sound professional but Geoff's whoop at the other end of the phone made it clear such restraint was unnecessary.

"Well done. Now get home safely and bring it over tomorrow morning and park where you normally do. I'll meet you there."

Mark parked the Transit on the road outside Feargal's house and on disembarking threw the keys to Feargal.

"There's no way I'm missing this tomorrow! What time are we leaving?"

"Let's leave at 8.30. I'll see you here."

Within moments his parents were outside and viewing the Transit from behind.

"Oh dear," said his father, "Oh dear me."

The journey up to court from Brixton was a difficult one for Pat that Wednesday. A lorrydriver had jack-knifed earlier in the day somewhere up beyond the turn off for St Albans and had added a good forty minutes to the travelling time. On top of this he had two travelling prisoners with him both about to start their trials for an armed robbery that had gone wrong. Normally he would have shared his experience with them and chatted enthusiastically about their cases but today he was not in the mood. Moreover his usual travelling guard with whom he had created a good working relationship was off and his replacement appeared sullen and unhelpful. Overnight Pat had decided that he would not give evidence unless things were going horribly wrong and would trust to good fortune with the jury visit and the arrival of the Transit.

It was the Transit that became the star act of the morning. The judge was notified by the defence team that the defendant wished the jury to see the van and Antrim-Davies could see no reason why they shouldn't. Consequently the court staff, aided by two local traffic policemen beckoned Feargal eventually to park in the road adjacent to the court building which allowed the jury with three ushers in close attendance to inspect the vehicle closely.

Pat was not allowed to attend but Chambers and the team were all there and were encouraged at the activity of the jurors, two of whom inspected the towbar closely and one of whom actually looked inside the bonnet and door panels to verify that the Transit was indeed originally blue and had not at any time been sprayed white.

Effectively that was the end of the defence evidence. The jury set off to Stetchworth after an early lunch and the circus resumed at the gun location. The jury coach had attracted the attention of all of the local kids, none of whom appeared to have gone to school that day. There were a lot of Stetchworth mothers in attendance too. For Feargal came total vindication as one juror after another attempted to access the place where the dummy shotgun in a sack had been positioned only to retreat from a thorny encounter or find their sleeves snagged on a branch. Almost without exception they came back to the coach brushing their jacket arms to remove real or imagined debris.

Thus only the closing speeches and the judge's summing up remained.

Ableman began early on the Thursday session. He was methodical and precise. Yes it was true that there was no 'smoking gun' in this case and it had been hard to discover a motive but, he assured the jury, that was not unusual. In cases like this it was the result of good police work and the piecing together of various seemingly unconnected clues that would lead them conclusively to the point where beyond any reasonable doubt the finger of guilt pointed at one man and one man only and that was Patrick Crehan.

The defendant seemed to be pleading a conspiracy of lies against him. Was it really conceivable that Mrs Appletree, that little old lady with the bad sciatica, would make up a sighting that was so damning for no reason or that John Graham and Ray Johnson would concoct a story about a shotgun to implicate the defendant? That was just too far-fetched, even in these modern times where conspiracy theories seemed to thrive. And then four separate police officers at different positions in their careers and lives. Why would they all make up their statements and perjure themselves. What did they have personally against the defendant? Nothing at all.

Mr O'Neill's evidence had fully linked the defendant with Graham. He acknowledged that he may have got the colour of his jumper wrong, or you may think that Mr Graham had mistaken the colour... he wasn't good with colours after all, and had mistaken the colour of Crehan's Transit for white, when everyone now accepted it was blue and always had been. He contended that he could read the number plate. Perhaps he was closer than he thought. It was suggested he might still be suffering the aftereffects of his bad accident, but you saw his demeanour. He seemed a perfectly reliable witness to me.

Miss Austin had simply cleared out the defendant's cell on instructions. She hadn't planted the chewing gum wrappers, had she?

And DS Jones and DC Barlow, what of their evidence? They had simply listened in to a conversation which showed that Graham and the defendant had something to hide. If their evidence had been concocted too, then why wasn't it far more damning. They could have lied to have the defendant admitting to the shooting, but they did not. They confined their evidence to exactly what they had heard. Perhaps their spelling was not good but it wasn't on trial here.

Finally he turned to the evidence of the Wednesday. You heard the evidence of the rather excitable young man who had attended the scene where the shotgun was found. He seemed to think that it was obvious that the defendant could not have hidden the gun in its position without there being a ton of forensic evidence on the defendant's coat. But remember, he was viewing the scene in July and the allegation is that the gun was placed there on November 6th in the early hours, in the winter when there would be no foliage. And yes, the experienced forensic officer made no mention of debris on the coat, no surprise you may think, but what he did find was the toxic print of shotgun discharge on that very coat… far more likely than the random discharge from an exhaust pipe wouldn't you think?

It is a very harsh task that you have in front of you. Nobody wishes to have the responsibility of sentencing a fellow human to what will inevitably entail a very long stretch of imprisonment. But you must be strong and bear in mind that a man was brutally killed, his young wife widowed and his children orphaned by that dreadful act in the early hours of November 6th last year.

You must steel yourselves to your duty and find this man guilty of Tony Blake's cold-blooded murder.

Ableman sat down and the Judge ordered a short coffee break.

"We'll leave you alone to compose your thoughts, Pat. I see no reason not to deliver exactly the same speech as we went through last night. Just be yourself. Good luck."

"Ladies and gentlemen of the jury. I am not a saint. You know that already. Far from it. I have been involved in crime since I was a teenager and before and I am not proud of it. I will never commit another crime. Look where it has landed me. I have a lovely wife who has stuck with me through all my badness and continues to be there for me. I have two lovely children and they deserve better.

"But I am not a murderer and I did not kill Tony Blake. On the night he died I was at home in bed with my wife. I had no reason to want Tony Blake dead. He was not a nice man. He had many enemies in Stetchworth and elsewhere but I was not one of those enemies.

"First of all, you may be wondering why I decided to dispense with the services of my learned counsel so early in these proceedings. Mr Salpetre is a brilliant QC. His reputation is unrivalled. But he wanted to run my defence using conventional techniques and my defence I believed, required anything but those techniques. You see. I know I did not commit this murder, or hire a gun to do it with and, knowing that, I realized that I was going to be forced to accuse everybody or almost everybody who gave evidence against me, of lying. We all know the story of 'The Little Boy who Cried Wolf' and I felt it was best that I cried wolf rather than my QC who was reluctant to.

"Before you consider the evidence with me, I would just like you to explore an absolutely outlandish idea with me. It will challenge your view of the very society in which you live but, and I apologise in advance for rocking your world, consider this.

"You will recall DCS Oliver refusing to name the 'reliable informant' who had given my name as the person who had committed this murder. I pressed him on this and you will recall the judge protecting him from divulging the name of the informant. Let's get real, members of the jury, I doubt if Oliver even knows who gave him my name but it was a start for him.

"Several days pass in the investigation and no further evidence has come out of the woodwork to suggest I was involved. What do we need? Well, first of all we need a gun and we have a fair idea that it was a 12-bore that killed Tony. We didn't find a 12-bore at Crehan's so let's connect him with one. Who can we lean on to say they gave Crehan the means of the murder? Oh, hang on a minute, what have we got on John Graham? Or Ray Johnson? Lock them up for a day or two and their addiction will have every sinew in their abused bodies crying out for the next fix. They will do anything to cooperate.

"So what do we end up with? A mystery gun supplier in Ware… members of the jury did you hear any evidence from a gun supplier in Ware? No. Of course not. They will have done a deal with him. He sells a shotgun to Ray Johnson… still absolutely no connection to me, and he sells it on to Graham who is willing to perjure himself and lob me in. God knows what they threatened him with, but as you know, he met me in my White transit van, which you all now know is actually blue in Bedwell, when, coincidence upon coincidence, Paddy O'Neill, newly out of hospital from a brain-threatening trauma, not only spots Graham coming out of my Transit from 50 yards, wearing a jumper, maybe red maybe blue, but also identifies the van from its number plate using modern memory enhancing techniques despite the fact that, as you have seen for yourselves, the number plate was totally indecipherable to the human eye other than up close and personal.

"It's all beyond belief to me. But do you understand why I am asking you to consider the ridiculous suggestion that your good old honest British police force is actually carrying out this travesty of justice.

"If I may, I'd like to go a few more steps with you. Let's consider the evidence of the three Stetchworth officers.

"First Austin. Isn't it just a bit too much of a stretch to believe that the fact that I chewed some Wrigley's gum in the 72 hours of my detention in the cells could possibly link me with the killing because some similar wrappers were found at the scene of the crime? Let's extend that with the thought of how many cul-de-sacs in Stetchworth, let alone England, have Wrigley's wrappers discarded in them? And how many cells.? The link is preposterous but it does show how absolutely desperate those conducting the investigation were to establish further bits of circumstantial evidence.

"Then Jones and Barlow… well I do not want to insult your intelligence but it could not be any clearer that the two of them got together to compile their statements. Of course they did. I actually don't mind that they broke all the rules in doing that. So far as I am concerned their version of what was said is not damaging to me at all, even though, as John Graham made clear to you, it bore no resemblance to what was actually said. For my sins I am a fairly hardened petty criminal. I know how the police behave in the cells. Had I wanted to, I could have produced extensive evidence from my defence team of the lengths they and I will go to in order not to be listened to in the cells or interview rooms. All I wanted Graham to do was be quiet,…. for his own and my sake, because I had already sussed what was taking place.

"Let's discuss the shotgun. This is interesting. No link has been made between the gun that Ray Johnson bought from the mystery dealer in Ware with the shotgun that was found by the kids in mid-November. And no link has been found between the shotgun found and the murder weapon. So we are in the unsatisfactory position where we do not even know that the weapon found was the murder weapon or whether the weapon I was supposed to have bought from the Ware dealer via Graham via Johnson was either the murder weapon or the one found. You might find even more interesting the fact that if you draw a straight line from the scene of the murder to my house, the location of the shotgun discovered is precisely halfway along that line… you couldn't make it up could you.? And you all attended that scene. Young Feargal wasn't excitable he was just telling the truth wasn't he?

"So how can we embellish upon that further? Ah yes, I know. We will go and find a neighbour somewhere along the route who saw me coming home at the time of the murder. What's more we haven't found a shotgun yet so they had better see him carrying something. Poor old Mrs Appletree. Her sciatica was playing her up. I hope none of you suffer from it, it is excruciatingly painful. And five days later she has it suggested to her that she saw me out of the window, and carrying something, at 2 am. Really! Can you remember what you were doing five nights ago? Or was it 6? Or was it 4?

"And one last thought….if I had hidden the alleged murder weapon where it was found after the murder and on my way straight home, how could Mrs Appletree have seen me hiding it under my arm? Doesn't really add up, does it?

"Members of the jury, I do not have to prove my innocence. In order to convict me you must believe beyond any reasonable doubt that on the night of November 5th and 6th last year for no reason that has been given, I, a man who has never shot a gun in his life, lay in wait for Tony Blake and in the presence of his poor wife mercilessly gunned him down. I think you can see that I was not that man and moreover you can see that the prosecution have failed miserably to prove their case. Please let me go home to my wife and try to be a better man. Thank you."

Antrim-Davies delivered his summing up perfectly. Known as a hanging judge he was well aware that any perverse comments would lead to an instant appeal, particularly by the defence in the event of a conviction, and so he led the jury once more, piece by piece through the evidence, pointing out all inconsistencies and stressing both sides of every contention. Eventually at 1.35 he sent them away to consider their verdict. Pat was returned to his cell and for the defence boys the long wait began.

Chambers treated them to a late lunch at the Tudor barns opposite and thanked each of the team for their efforts. No one discussed the case or the likely verdict. They didn't want to jinx anything. At 4.30pm the judge called the jury in and asked the foreman if they were close to a verdict. They were not and after a second call in at 6 pm the judge sent the jury away and ordered they be sequestered for the night, to resume at 9.30 am the following morning.

It was 11am the following morning and one of the hottest days of the year. Pat Crehan sat alone in his cell. He had managed little sleep last night, tossing and turning over whether he had done it right. Should he have said this, not said that? He was full of doubt and had rather snapped at Bridget when she had first arrived with a clean shirt and tie and freshly pressed suit. He regretted it and had quickly made amends with a cuddle and reassuring words. Poor Bridget, what a torture this must have been for her.

The warder assigned to him had been most kind all morning. He had done this many times he told Pat and there was nothing he could do but hold fast and believe. He even had one of the junior crown court staff go out and return with jam doughnuts for Pat, which at least lightened the atmosphere.

Outside the court, the defence team had yet again taken over the small consultation room positioned at the exit to the court. Understandably they were in pensive mood. Chambers in particular was very quiet. Steve and Feargal chatted from time to time, Steve providing a running commentary on how long the jury had been out. Both had agreed that the judge had left little by way of material grounds for appeal, at least Steve said that and Feargal agreed with him. He had after all never been involved in a major trial before.

Geoff left the court buildings for a smoke at around 12.30 having funded up Feargal to go and get the sandwich orders for lunch. Before he went he chatted with Steve.

"What do you think?"

"You can never tell but a long deliberation usually means that at least someone in that jury room is digging her or his heels in."

"Here's hoping. I thought the big guy at the back with grey hair looked very pissed off with Jones and Barlow."

"Yeah, he couldn't hide it could he. Trouble is you don't know why he was annoyed. Could be he believed what they had done but knew they were lying about the notebooks…"

"What happens with a hung jury?"

"Retrial or acquittal by the judge, but Marcus won't acquit."

"So retrial?"

At 2.30 the judge summoned the jury back and addressed the foreman, who happened to be the same large man with grey hair who Feargal and Steve had discussed.

"I've called you back to see how you are progressing. Are you close to reaching a verdict upon which you are all agreed?"

"No, your Honour."

"Very well, I am now allowed to direct you to please go and continue your discussions but I am able now to accept a verdict upon which at least ten of you are agreed. Obviously I would like you to try and reach unanimity but I am prepared to take a verdict where ten or eleven of you are agreed. Is that clear?"

"Yes, your Honour" Most of the jury nodded.

The jury filed back into their room at the side of the court and the waiting began again.

At 17 minutes past 5, news was passed to the team that the jury were coming back. The judge had not summoned them in so far as anyone knew so this must either be a verdict or a request for some direction.

Again the judge asked if a unanimous verdict had been reached and the foreman answered in the negative.

"Very well, Have you reached a verdict upon which at least ten of you agreed?'

"Yes we have Your Honour."

The judge looked at Mrs James.

She rose and addressed the foreman.

"On the charge of the murder of Anthony Blake on the 6th November 1972, how do you find the defendant, Patrick Crehan, guilty or not guilty?"

An age passed. At the back of the courtroom at one end Bridget sat with her face covered and a friend's arms around her shoulders. At the other end of the gallery, not 20 yards from her sat Jo Blake and a few others.

"Not guilty."

Epilogue

Time moved on from that momentous Friday afternoon at St Albans Crown Court. For those involved it marked the date from which all circumstantial police-gathered evidence was viewed with huge suspicion and mistrust. No longer could the police force rely on the natural assumption of guilt once they had seen fit to bring charges.

For the defence team it was also a turning point in their young lives. Geoffrey Chambers was soon to cease making criminal practice his bread and butter. His marriage foundered and within six months he was living with the daughter of a probation officer near Carlisle and enjoying an existence caring for young children and defending good causes. His talents as a lawyer were however nationally recognized and before long he was the go-to lawyer for the Greenpeace foundation.

Steve Evans too found that his home relationship had been compromised over the period of the trial. He moved on to another partner in due course and another law firm where he forged a reputation as one of the best welfare lawyers around, protecting the wellbeing of the underprivileged and abused wherever he practiced.

Feargal went on to do his degree at Oxford where he worked little and played a lot, often aided by the group from the Cromwell. His confidence in himself never deserted him and it was only much later in life that he realized that while such self-belief could carry people with him, it could also be damaging to relationships. He eventually qualified as a solicitor but chose to go overseas to practice.

And what of Pat? He returned home that evening to be greeted by well-wishers and friends. Within a few days however, Bridget had left with the children for some time away. Nobody ever spoke of the reasons behind her leaving. She was never to return.

Pat bought himself a taxi licence and applied himself to a daily routine of taxi driving around Stetchworth. It was a strange choice for someone who had been so much in the public eye, but he enjoyed it and liked the catharsis of discussing the case with anyone who recognized him and cared to put in a supportive word

The night of November 5th would be a strange one and he found himself at the front of the rank just behind the Edward the Confessor Pub in Danestrete. It was a dank and miserable night and no customers were in view.

The back door clicked open and a 50-something male pulled himself into the back.

"Yes, where to Guv?"

"I'd like to go to the Bowie Club out past Hitchin if you can?" the man said in an Irish brogue.

"Yes, I know it well as it happens."

They drove in silence for most of the journey, but as they were passing through the outskirts of Hitchin, Pat volunteered,

"So how are things?"

"Ah you know, still being cheated by my old employers. They still owe me for my accident. I guess they'll never learn."

"You're recovered now though?"

"Ahh to be sure, fit as a flea and happy with it. How's life with you?"

"Oh, can't complain."

As they drew into the car park at the Bowie Club, the passenger spoke again.

"You know, it's a filthy night and there won't be many fares around. I'm meeting a few friends. Will you join us for one?"

"That sounds like fun," said Pat turning off the ignition.

They exited the car and went over to the neon entrance of the Bowie Club and pushed open the door. It was only 8.30 pm but there were already a few people inside. Pat held the door open and his passenger went on inside. They took off their outer clothes and embraced the warm embrace of men who had a collective intent.

Paddy waved to John Graham and Ray Johnson who raised their drinks in greeting.